Boo

C000183931

Coyote's Kiss
Wolf Pack

Bloodlines

Bite

Bite Me!

Savage Love

Summer Seductions

Summers' Girl

Cloaks and Daggers

Vampire Hunter

Lust Bites

Seduced by the Neighbour
Fated Love
Bid High
Lacey's Seduction

What's Her Secret?

Designated Alpha
Last Call

Single Titles

Eternal
Magical Ménage
Vamps in the City

Pack Enforcer

ISBN # 978-1-78686-061-3

Cover Art by Posh Gosh ©Copyright 2016

Interior text design by Claire Siemaszkiewicz

Totally Bound Publishing

Published in 2016 by Totally Bound Publishing, Newland House, The Point, Weaver Road, Lincoln, LN6 3QN, United Kingdom.

Totally Bound Publishing is a subsidiary of Totally Entwined Group Limited.

Were Chronicles

PACK ENFORCER

CRISSY SMITH

Dedication

This book goes to everyone who loves the wolves — thanks for the support. It's been such an awesome ride and I hope you enjoy the new content.

Chapter One

Emily Black kicked her shoes off and laughed as they flew across her living room. *Godforsaken things.* It felt so good to be barefoot. She hated shoes no matter what kind they were. At least the tennis shoes she wore to class were more comfortable than the heels her friends wore. She couldn't even imagine how much her girlfriends' feet ached after hoofing it across campus. Even though classes weren't in session, as the new semester hadn't yet started, Emily had spent the day going over her options for her upcoming schedule, trying to decide if she wanted to make any changes. She'd brought home the selections her counsellor had given her and she planned to choose in the next couple of days.

She nudged her shoes under the coffee table then stripped off her shirt and jeans while heading into the bedroom for loose shorts and a tank top. Once comfortable, she strolled to the kitchen. The fridge, which she kept overstocked, was cool as she opened it. She grabbed a bottle of water and the Tupperware full of lasagna she had made last night. She placed the container in the microwave then punched in two minutes at high heat. As she waited with the fork in her hand, she jumped up onto the counter.

A human would consider her behavior weird or think that she hadn't eaten in hours. But for her, it was just another day. She had eaten lunch only two hours ago, but a shifter burned a lot of energy and needed to eat large regular meals, especially when the full moon was close. All her hungers increased as the natural cycle for shifters approached.

She, however, ate many small meals. Especially around

the few people she called her friends. All the girls and guys who she hung around with were human and they wouldn't understand what she hid behind closed doors. No one at school knew about her shifter abilities. Of that she was pretty sure. To them, she was just a quiet girl who liked to study and keep to herself. She was pretty in a traditional way, but not a head-turner. She would leave being stunning and charming to those around her. She preferred to blend in and not draw attention to herself.

Her blinking answering machine light caught her eye, but she wasn't in any hurry to check. It was probably someone trying to sell her something. She didn't get many phone calls. All her true friends were back in Pack territory and they usually called on the weekends. She missed them, but was still proud that she'd gotten accepted to the state university a couple of hours away from Pack land.

When she'd first made the decision to attend college out of Pack territory, she'd never thought it would be so hard to be away from them. The longer she stayed in the city, the more her mind drifted back to her friends and family. And the man who her heart belonged to.

The microwave dinged and she yanked the handle to open it up. Even though the food was still steaming, she started to shovel it into her mouth. She was getting better at cooking and this recipe was one of her very favorites. When the container was half empty, Emily finally took a deep breath and set it down, giving her stomach time to process the food she'd practically inhaled.

She hopped off the counter to walk over to the cabinet next to the fridge and grabbed the leftover rolls she'd put in a plastic baggie. As she passed the answering machine she hit the play button.

"Hello, Emily dear."

Emily smiled at hearing her Alpha's voice. The man she thought of as a father and trusted above all else.

"I know you have a lot going on right now. Thank you for the email with your final grades. I am very proud of you."

She always kept him apprised of what was going on with her classes. He was paying for her education, after all.

"Something happened, not here but close by, I need to make sure you're all right. Please call me right away."

The last part was an order, and Emily could hear it even over the phone line. She shivered slightly just from the demand. As close as she was to Lamont, he was still her leader and she was obligated to follow his orders. Not that Emily argued with him often. He accused her of being too stubborn for her own good sometimes, but he always said it with love. God, she missed him.

Thinking about her Alpha always brought up the person who she would never be able to forget. When she closed her eyes at night it was always *him* that she saw in her dreams. Just because she'd never have him didn't keep Emily from fantasizing about Lamont's son Cain.

Cain was the Pack Enforcer. A job that kept him busy, and over the years had made him tough but wary. He had a lot of the same duties as a Beta, the Alpha's second, but in addition was the top guard. Not every Pack had an Enforcer, but theirs did because it was so large. Cain was the number one guy in protecting Pack members and he took his job seriously. He'd always made sure that Emily was safe. Even if he didn't feel the same way about her as she did about him.

Emily went back to the counter then picked up her leftover food and water bottle before strolling into the living room. She set the items on the coffee table as she sat on the couch. "Let's get this over with," she muttered, leaning over to pick up the cordless phone on the end table. She dialed her Alpha and waited.

* * * *

Cain knocked on the door to his Alpha's study and waited for the grunt meaning it was okay to come in. He entered and remained silent as Lamont finished his phone call. If Lamont hadn't wanted the conversation overheard, he wouldn't have let Cain in. Werewolf hearing was better than any device you could buy. With the extra soundproofing throughout the entire house, Cain only heard the other side of the conversation his Alpha was having because he was in the room.

Cain immediately recognized the young were's voice on the other end of the line. She spoke softly to the Alpha of the Pack, although her tone showed frustration. Hearing her sent a shiver trailing down Cain's spine, and a jolt to his cock had him hardening. He quickly cut down that train of thought, which would lead him to imagining the things that he wanted to do to Emily Black. She was so far out of his league that he had to forget about her. Let her live her own life and stay far, far away. It would be a lot easier if he knew she was safe.

They all worried about the young were women who were out of the Pack's territory. In all of the attacks that had recently taken place, the females had been away from home. Showing why he was Alpha, Lamont was calling them home before Cain had thought of it. He wanted to hug his Alpha, thankful that Emily's safety was being taken care of. He'd always watched out for the young woman when she'd been inside the Pack, but he had limited resources when dealing with trouble on the outside.

"Have some bags packed when your ride gets there," Lamont said sternly into the phone.

Cain barely held back a smile when he heard the order. Lamont was putting his foot down and Emily would have to obey.

"No, someone will be there to pick you up." He looked over at Cain. "It will be someone you recognize from the Pack. Do not leave with anyone else."

Lamont listened for a few more minutes before cutting her off. "No. You will stay in one of the cabins. It will be fully furnished for your arrival." He waited again. "You'll stay until we know what is going on and I tell you it's okay to go back." That was all Alpha speaking to one of his Pack. Cain knew how Lamont felt about Emily. How everyone felt.

Emily had been found in a cage when she was a young girl. No one knew what birth Pack she was from and they'd never found her family. Even the Alpha Council, a group of Alphas who helped police Packs and keep them safe from humans, hadn't been able to track down where Emily came from. It was Cain's grandfather who had come across the house of rogue wolves who'd been keeping young shifters caged. None of the rogues had made it out of the rescue alive and the children had all been sent to foster Packs. Emily had been placed with them, which had led to her and Cain growing up together, since he was only a few years older than her.

He turned his attention to the man who sat behind the desk. A man he respected more than anyone else.

"You know that was Emily," Lamont told him once he hung up the phone.

"She's coming home?" Cain asked even though he knew the answer.

Lamont nodded at him. "I want every female home and safe. I knew it would be difficult to convince her, but she finally agreed."

Cain didn't understand why he didn't just order her home and be done with it. He was her Alpha and for everything that they'd done for her, Emily should always listen to her Alpha. It was what being a good shifter was all about. Cain strived to be the best shifter he could but Emily had an independent streak a mile wide. It was why she needed so much protection.

She'd been twelve when she'd been brought home to the Pack. While he'd always tried to keep her out of trouble, it wasn't an easy task, made harder by the feelings that had developed for her. He was frustrated, but knew that he would feel much better if she'd just come home. At least

11

he was getting that wish…for now. Once they could ensure her safety living outside the Pack, he'd once again have to let her go.

"I want you to go get her and bring her here safely," Lamont told him.

Cain merely stared at his Alpha. No, he couldn't do that. He would do anything for his Pack, his Alpha, but that was asking too much. He couldn't outright refuse, though. "Me? You sure? Maybe Tony would be better," he suggested instead.

Lamont looked at his second-in-command and raised an eyebrow. The look clearly said that he would not be questioned on this topic.

Cain cleared his throat. "Of course. I'll leave right away." He turned to walk out.

"Cain," Lamont called after him. He waited until Cain had turned around and met his gaze. "I know there's something between you and Emily that you are trying to fight. I've given you both time to sort through your feelings and have not interfered. Do you want to discuss it?"

Cain shook his head. This was the last thing he'd expected to have to talk about. He'd been so careful not to let anyone pick up on his feelings for Emily. If his Alpha had a suspicion, then did the others? "I don't know what you're talking about." There, if he didn't admit to anything he wouldn't have to have this conversation.

Lamont stood and walked around the desk. "I'm not asking as your Alpha. I'm asking as your father. You can talk to me. You know I'll help you in any way possible."

What could he share with his Alpha, his father, that wouldn't have him looking like a complete asshole? He was a dominant male. Emily was still young and had already been through so much. He couldn't subject her to the kind of control that he had to have in his relationships. That wouldn't be fair to her. She'd already proven that she wouldn't just let him do the protecting and stay at his back. Several years ago she'd demanded that he train her to fight. Lamont had taken her side and ordered him to teach her. Cain had done his best to get her to change her mind but Emily wouldn't back off. He'd eventually began to meet with her every morning in the gym and share his knowledge with her.

It was the longest year Cain could ever remember in his life. The attraction that had been blooming between the two of them had seemed to sizzle and burn even hotter. The first time he'd touched her to show her a throw, there had been a spark. He could still remember the moment. The widening of her eyes, the catch of her breath and the feel of her skin under his hands. He had backed away immediately, but the damage had been done. The attraction had been noted and they both knew it.

But the big episode had come at the end of a year of working with her. She'd been eighteen by then, but still off-limits to him. She deserved so much better than the life he could provide her and he wouldn't hold her back from following her dreams. He had made a promise to protect her, and he would — even from him.

She had just thrown him, and he kicked the back of her knee, having her go down at the same time. He shifted to break her fall, and her body fell onto his. She didn't rush or scramble off him as she should have.

Their eyes met, and there was that connection once again. Then her mouth was on his, moist and hesitant. It was a feeling he would never forget. Her lips moving and caressing while her hand rubbed his chest. He rolled her onto her back, taking control of the kiss, deepening it, making it hard and rough. He slid his hands under her tank top and rubbed her breasts, pulling at her nipples as he kissed her mouth. She moaned and he felt that into the deepest core of his body. He was between her legs, hard as a rock and ready to plunge into her the moment he could pull her shorts off.

He stroked down from her breasts, past her stomach, to her hot core. He slipped his hand into her shorts and inside her panties, skimming his fingers against liquid heat. As he brushed his hand

over her pussy, she pressed against it, begging him to take her.
And as she moaned and writhed under his touch, the kiss became
brutal. When he dipped his finger inside, she exploded and rocked
while screaming at the climax that tore through her body.

He shook the memory away. He hadn't handled that well. He had come to his senses at the last minute. He'd stopped before it was too late, sent her back to the house and avoided her from then on. After that, she'd begged and pleaded with Lamont to let her go away to college.

Neither Lamont nor Cain had wanted to let her go. Being in Pack territory almost guaranteed her safety. Lamont had held off as long as he'd been able to, had kept her there for four years at the community college two towns over.

Finally, he'd had to let her go to complete her final years of education. At twenty-two, she'd left to go to the closest university. They still worried with her being outside the territory, but she had promised one thing.

If trouble came, if she got a call from the Alpha, she would return home.

The call had come now, and Cain would be the one to pick her up.

She'd returned every summer and for holidays to spend her time off with the only family she had ever known or could remember. So they had been thrown together numerous times but had managed to avoid each other and talking about what happened.

Obviously, they hadn't avoided keeping everything from the Alpha. From his father.

"No, nothing to talk about. I can assure you." Cain shook his head.

Lamont didn't look convinced, but nodded. "Then go get our girl."

Cain turned and left to go get her. He could guarantee that Emily would not be happy to see him and it was going to be a long fucking ride back.

He stomped through the Alpha house, ignoring the looks he received from other Pack members. If he left now, he could grab Emily and get her back tonight. He did not want to stay in the city, and there was no way in hell he could spend the night in her apartment.

It was just an order by his Alpha that he had to follow. He had no choice and neither did she. A couple of hours on the road and he'd have her back into the safety of the Pack and he could go back to avoiding her.

A simple task that he would fulfill.

As he stepped out of the front door to his vehicle, Cain knew he was kidding himself. As soon as they were locked together in the car her scent would be all over him. It would take every ounce of control he had to keep his hands off her.

Cain jogged forward, praying that he could keep his vow to himself.

Chapter Two

At the knock on the door, Emily glanced up. She had been sitting on her couch with her packed bags at her feet. It seemed like she'd been waiting for hours, although in reality, by the time she'd called a few friends and cleaned up her apartment, she'd had to rush to pack her bags. Emily had told those she'd spoken to that she'd had a family emergency that required her to go out of town. At least the university offered several online options she could take advantage of if she didn't make it back in time for the beginning of classes. She just hoped that once the threat against her and the other females had passed she'd be able to come back.

She was twenty-two and it was time for her to let silly dreams of Mr. Right go and concentrate on what she wanted. And she wanted to finish her education so she would be a valuable member of the Pack that had taken her in.

The knock sounded again and she smiled. Nothing like an impatient wolf at the door. She opened up, still smiling until she got a look at the dark, handsome man standing there.

Damn.

Cain looked wonderful. He was over six feet tall with black hair and gold eyes. His hair was longer than she remembered and fell over his forehead. Her fingers twitched to push it back. She couldn't do that, though. Cain wouldn't allow her touch. But with him standing there in front of her, all those feelings that she'd tried to bury came rushing back up to the surface. He radiated strength as he leaned against the threshold, and she wondered, not for the first time, how he could be so calm.

His eyes seemed to be taking her in the same way as she was him.

"Surprised?" he asked, with a nasty twist of his lip. His voice was hard, just like it had been for the past several years. It hurt that he couldn't look at her like he'd once done and that they couldn't joke around. They'd once been friends, but now he acted like he couldn't stand to be in the same room with her. Damn, she'd screwed everything up. Regret burned over the shock of seeing him. Time hadn't made her care any less or not want him. This close, she could see the strain in his features. Emily actually had to curl her fist to keep from running her thumb over the dark circles under his eyes.

If these feelings inside were any indication, then she wasn't over this handsome, cocky wolf in front of her. It was going to be a long drive and they both knew it. She opened the door wider to allow him in. "I was expecting Tony."

"Well, you got me instead." Cain stepped into the small apartment. Without turning back to her, Cain strolled through the living room, not even hiding that he was sniffing the air.

"What are you doing?" she asked as her eyes narrowed. Even though she knew exactly what he was doing. Okay, maybe she didn't *know* but she suspected he was scenting for other men. He'd always done that around her. But she hadn't been 'dating' anyone recently, so there were no other scents in her apartment but hers.

At one time, Emily had believed he did it because he cared, was jealous or something. Now she'd figured he only did it because he was a control freak. "Well?" she pressed.

He just smiled back at her. He rocked back on his heels then stuffed his hands in his front pockets.

"Ugh." She stomped over to her two bags and picked them up. "Fine, let's go." If he was going to act like an irritating ass then she would just have to ignore him. That would drive him crazy. Cain had no problem not speaking to her but he seemed to also want her attention on him. She wasn't going to give him what he wanted this time, though. Once they got on the road she wouldn't have to talk to him at all.

Cain's eyes lit in amusement, which made him look years younger. It was such a rare treat that she just stood and stared at him. What was happening? Maybe he was coming down sick or something. That was the only reason she could think of. "Cain?"

He shook his head before the serious expression of an Enforcer reappeared. Of course, she should have expected it, but his reaction hurt.

"Is there anything you want to say?" she asked. Could he be ready to talk about what had happened between them?

Cain only grunted as he strode his way over to her and yanked her bags out of her hands. He nodded toward the door. "After you."

Emily huffed to hide her disappointment. Even when she was pissed off at him she still craved his touch. She stepped past him, making sure they didn't touch. There was no way she could keep herself under control if she touched him. She'd made a fool of herself once and that had been bad enough. She wouldn't repeat her mistake.

She didn't say a word to him as she stomped into the hall and turned to wait for him to follow. As soon as he was over the threshold, Emily slammed the door closed and locked it. She absolutely was not going to talk to him as long as he was acting like an asshole. Cain was already striding down the walkway to the stairs so she had to hurry and catch up with him before he bitched about her not moving quickly enough.

* * * *

It took Emily twenty minutes in the car to finally give in. Cain knew she would. She always made the first attempt to talk. This time was no different.

"Why am I going back?" she asked.

"That's where you belong," Cain told her, tightening his hands on the wheel. He believed that with all his heart even if it wasn't the reason that she was returning.

She snorted. "Says you, but Lamont wouldn't have called me back without a good reason."

Cain glanced over at the woman next to him. It had taken all the control he had not to grab her in his arms the moment she'd opened the door. She was everything he remembered, everything he dreamed of at night. He could swear her scent had wrapped him into a web when he'd first seen her. But his job was to protect her and he didn't want her afraid of him. Weighing his options, he decided to tell her as little as possible.

"There have been some attacks on female weres outside Pack territory," he said gently.

When her eyes widened with horror, he reached over and patted her leg. The moment that he touched her, Cain realized his mistake. The spark that he'd felt before ignited and he yanked his hand back, quickly trying to cover his gasp. *Fuck, that was stupid.* He cleared his throat. "No one in our Pack. It's been four women so far, but Lamont wants to be careful. The latest one was from Christian's Pack."

She shivered. He didn't know if it was from his touch or his words. It was better that he didn't know.

"Who?" she asked quietly.

He frowned, thinking he should have left this for Lamont. Cain just knew he'd fuck this up some way. But he'd started down this road and she did deserve to know about the danger. Forget about not telling her everything to protect her. The more information she had, the better Emily could protect herself in case he wasn't close by. "Mindy."

She turned and looked out at the passing scenery. "What happened to her?"

"You don't need to know that," he said. That wasn't something that she needed to think about.

"Cain," she said. "I think that since I was called home due to it being a danger to me, and the fact that a good friend was attacked only two territories over, I should have a good idea of what is going on. I'm a big girl, I can handle it."

"No," he said. "You don't need the details. What's important is that there is a threat and you will be taken care of. Nothing will happen to you," he promised. "If you want to hit up Lamont for that information, that's fine, but I'm not telling you." He took a deep breath. This was harder than he'd expected.

Deep down, he knew she had the right to know. But the details of the attack would be hard to deal with. Emily had been through so much and she didn't deserve to be hunted or hurt. Finding out what was happening to the other females would hurt her too.

"Just tell me if she's okay," she pleaded.

Cain couldn't even give her that because he didn't know. He reached over, turned the radio on then put both hands on the wheel. He prayed this drive would go fast. With a firm grip on the steering wheel, he pressed his foot down harder on the accelerator, hoping to make it back home as quickly as possible.

Emily just stared at him. She'd been dismissed. Just like that, he thought he could tell her that they weren't going to talk about it and they weren't. Well, he had another thing coming. She'd tried, she told herself. She would have been nice and polite, but his attitude just stank. She switched the radio off.

"Listen to me, Cain," she demanded, keeping her voice low and calm.

In obvious surprise, he glanced over at her immediately.

"I'm not a child any longer. You can't pat me on the head and send me to my room," she told him.

He cleared his throat. "I never did that."

She laughed. "Yes, you did. I made a pass at you, you turned me down. We are both adults, and I think it's time you stopped holding a grudge." It was past time for them to clear the air. How long was he going to hold that one incident against her? It wasn't fair and she missed her friend. Cain had been so important to her and she wanted him back in her life. Even if it couldn't be how she wished it to be.

In the years she'd been away at school she'd tried to forget him. Had had other relationships and tried to move on. One of the reasons she didn't think she'd been successful at that was because he had cut off all ties between them.

Emily could be strong and not come on to him again, but she didn't want to continue like they had been. It hadn't hit her that she felt this way until she'd seen him standing at her door earlier that night. "Just get over it so we can move on," she said as she turned her head to stare out of the window again.

"What are you talking about?" he asked sharply.

When she didn't say anything, he whipped the car to the shoulder of the highway and slammed on the brakes. She had to put her hands out in front of her to keep from hitting her head, and the seat belt tightened around her body.

"What the hell!" she cried out.

He undid his seat belt and turned to face her. "I hate to tell you that you're wrong, but being that you are, I'll force myself. I crossed a line with you. I shouldn't have, and I apologize. If the only way to make sure it doesn't happen again is to stay away from you, then I will."

His eyes were practically glowing. That wasn't the reaction that she'd expected. Why was he still angry with her? Yes, she'd fallen in love with him but as soon as he'd made his wishes known and had sent her away, Emily had never pressed him again. Cain should accept that.

"What line did you cross?" she asked gently, placing her hand on his arm. The way he'd angled himself put them within touching distance and she had to reach for him. Just this once as she figured out what he was talking about.

He growled in the back of his throat. "You know damn

well what I did."

She nodded, not moving her hand. "I know what you did, Cain, and I know what you didn't do."

He tried to pull away, but she tightened her grip. She might not be as strong or as fast, but in the confines of a car, he couldn't move enough to avoid her.

"You refused an eighteen-year-old girl who jumped on you, who had planned for months for the right moment to make her move. Maybe I made a mistake. I don't think I did, but I know you do. I was eighteen and infatuated with you, Cain. You were all I could think about. When you sent me back into the house, it broke my heart."

It was time for honesty. This had been going on with them for far too many years. "I'm still not sorry," she told him. "And you didn't do anything to be ashamed of. It was my doing. And"—she added with a small smile—"I can't promise I wouldn't do it again if I went back. No one's ever kissed me like that again."

He shook his head but his lips twitched in amusement. "You were a child."

She shook her head sadly. "I stopped being a child at twelve, Cain." She ran her gaze over him and felt warmth spread through her. God, she wished she could have him like she'd always wanted.

"That's no excuse," he told her. "I took advantage."

"How?" she asked. Emily had been there that day. She'd planned the scene over and over in her head a million times. Cain hadn't done anything wrong except for growing cold with her afterward. "I really want to know what you think you actually did."

He growled.

"Because it was me who pushed you into training me so I could be alone with you," she said. "I was the one who kissed you, if you'll remember. It was what I wanted and I never said no to you. I wouldn't have. *You* did."

"You had no idea what you were doing," Cain claimed.

"Are you kidding me!" she exclaimed. "I knew exactly

what I was doing. What I wanted from you. I almost got it too."

"You were too young to know anything," he said, but he didn't sound as sure as he normally did.

She blew out a breath. "Now who's wrong?" she asked.

He sputtered, but she shook her head.

"Maybe you need to think about what happened. If you remember the details you'll see the truth," she said.

"Like I haven't thought about that day a hundred times," he muttered.

"What?" she asked, shocked. He was constantly making her unsure of his feelings with comments like that. Either he wanted her or he didn't. It was that simple. Cain was so confident in every aspect of his life that she could not understand why he'd turned into such an asshole when he could have simply said no.

Cain didn't answer—he just straightened in his seat then pulled his seat belt back on. "We need to get back on the road."

"Sure," she scoffed. He wasn't listening to her any longer but at least she'd gotten to have her say. There was something in the way that he gripped the steering wheel until his knuckles turned white, while he was clenching his jaw, that made her see him in a new light.

Could he be scared? Thinking back on everything that he'd ever said to her since that night when she'd been eighteen made her think that she might be on to something.

Growing up, Cain had always considered it his job to protect her. Emily wasn't naïve enough to think it was because he didn't care—she knew he did. However, she might not be the only one who was sitting in the vehicle trying to fight their feelings.

From the corner of her eye, she watched him as she sat back more comfortably in her seat and crossed her legs. Right there! He was watching her back. Emily ran her hands down her thighs to grip her knees, trying to make the move seem as natural as possible. She didn't want to push him too far, but she was curious about how he'd react.

The scent of anger in the car was fading away and a stronger, sweeter smell replaced it. *Holy shit!* Cain was turned on.

How was it possible she'd missed these signs before? Yes, she had to admit. She'd been so broken up about Cain's rejection that she hadn't been around him much, and when she had been, Emily had fought to control her emotions from being apparent to him.

This turn of events was something she would definitely have to think about before doing anything that would end up getting her heart broken again. She was in love with Cain, but if he denied her again, Emily wasn't sure that she would recover. On the other hand, she finally had an opportunity to be in control of something between the two of them.

She crossed her arms over her chest, making sure to press her breasts out so he would have to notice.

Cain began to mutter under his breath as he punched at the radio dial to change the station.

Oh, this was very, very interesting.

It was one thing to play around, but she did have some serious thinking to do before she pushed Cain any further. If she wanted Cain, she was going to have to convince him that she was old enough and ready to settle down. His words earlier made that crystal clear. This time, she vowed, if she made her move she would not allow Cain push her away.

Chapter Three

Emily was still thinking about her breakfast with Lamont earlier as she made cookies with Toby, the youngest of the Alpha's children. Lamont hadn't held back the way Cain had the night before and had even shared more than she really wanted to know. She was hoping that spending time with the always-happy Toby would help get the images from her head.

It wouldn't hurt and she had the added benefit that no one would bring up the attacks around Toby. He was still too young to understand fully what was going on. Well, that wasn't true. He probably knew more than anyone else since he liked to sneak around and eavesdrop on his dad and brothers, but Emily didn't think he knew the horrible details.

Toby giggled as he stood over the tray they'd just taken out of the oven. He was practically drooling.

Eric, one of the guards, came in, and Emily smiled at him. She didn't know him well but they were friendly.

"Good morning," Emily greeted him.

"Something smells good," Eric said with a smile. He walked over to Toby and ruffled his hair.

Toby scowled at him as he swiped at his hands, but Eric easily dodged. "What's up, little man?"

"I'm not little!" Toby exclaimed with a frown.

At that moment, she could see how much Toby was growing up and that he was taking after Cain. She hid her smile behind a glass of milk so Toby wouldn't be irritated with her as he was with the guard.

"I think these are ready," Emily said hoping to bring a

smile back to Toby's face.

Emily set two cookies on a napkin for Toby and pushed them over before doing the same for Eric.

"How's school going?" Eric asked before he took a bite of his cookie.

"Really good," she answered.

"Staying long?" he asked next.

She shrugged then glanced toward Toby. "Not sure yet."

Eric nodded. "Maybe we can get together while you're here."

Was he really asking her out? Emily smiled. Since the incident with Cain, she hadn't really considered anyone else in the Pack as a hook-up. Sure, she was older now, but normally most of the males just treated her like a kid sister. It was flattering that Eric wanted to see her but there was only one man she wanted in the Pack.

"What's going on in here?"

Emily jumped, as did Eric, but Toby was grinning. She tried to calm her racing heart by taking deep breaths. It wasn't like she or Eric had been doing anything wrong.

Once she felt like she wouldn't freak out, Emily turned and plastered on a bright smile. "Eating cookies. Want some?" she asked. Damn, she should have kept her back turned. He looked fucking great in a pair of black slacks and a white button-down collared shirt with the sleeves rolled up. He looked more edible than the cookies.

Cain looked at the guard, who had straightened from behind her. "What kind?" He walked over and took one. "Eric," he said with a nod.

The coldness in his tone sent shivers down her spine. She didn't know if Cain had a problem with Eric, but it seemed like he did. Emily felt bad for Eric. She knew what it was like being on Cain's bad side but it would be a lot worse for a guard under Cain's control.

Eric cleared his throat. "Yeah, well, I better get back outside. Thanks for the cookies, Emily. See you later, Toby."

She smiled at him. "No problem."

"Bye," Toby said with his mouth full.

Now that it was just the three of them in the kitchen, Emily could feel the tension start to edge in. She had hoped that their talk last night would have made things better, but it didn't appear so. She sighed before turning back to the counter.

Cain stood close to her and she could feel irritation radiating off him. His arm brushed hers as he picked up a cookie. She stiffened. It was too early in the morning for this bullshit. And she had been having fun with Toby before Cain had decided to barge in.

"Cain," she said in warning as she turned to look at him. She had every right to be in the kitchen and he needed to get used to it.

He took another bite then said, "Go play outside, Toby," while still looking at her.

Toby frowned, glancing at his milk and cookies. "But I don't wanna."

Cain did look at Toby then, and had him scrambling up from his chair and out of the sliding glass door. Emily watched him go, preparing herself for round two with Cain. That hadn't been fair.

When the door finally slid back into place, she whirled around. "What is your problem now, Cain?"

She was prepared for a fight, not for being lifted off her feet and his lips against hers. She was so surprised her mouth opened in a gasp. He used that opening to slide his tongue in. It was rough and brutal and bruising. It was everything she wanted from him.

Emily pressed back against him, refusing to let him have complete control. A growl rose up from his chest but she didn't care. This was different from last time. *He'd* kissed *her* and she was not about to waste a minute. She wrapped her arms around his neck and her legs around his waist. His hard length pressed up against her. It made her moan and tighten her legs around him. Fuck, she wanted to feel him inside her. She hadn't gotten that before and she so wanted to have Cain claim her from the inside out. He left her mouth and continued kissing, nibbling her chin, her neck, her shoulder. She shuddered as she rocked and clawed at him.

Emily moaned, letting him know how much she wanted him. They couldn't stop this time. He had to follow through or she might die.

Cain leaned her back against the counter with one arm around her waist while he slipped his other hand under her shirt. Emily bit her lip to keep from crying out as he ran his fingers over the soft silk of her bra before pushing it away and finding her skin. His palm was hot and rough — perfect. She wanted to scream at how good his hand and mouth felt on her. Why didn't he just drag her to the floor and mount her like she was begging for him to?

"Please," she pleaded.

"Fuck!" he whispered before he was releasing her, sliding her back off the counter and turning her away from him. Stepping back, he put her hands on the counter and straightened her clothes from behind for her. She looked back at him, confused, hungry and hot.

"Cain."

He just shook his head and nodded to the kitchen door. Not a minute later, Tony walked in. Emily busied herself washing her hands, using the cold water to try to relieve the heat burning in her body.

When she turned around, Cain didn't even look at her as he ate the cookies, not quite pulling off the innocent look he was going for.

"Good God, are you two fighting again?" Tony said as he continued farther into the room. He walked over to the counter and popped a cookie in his mouth. "The emotions swirling around in this room are enough to strangle a man."

Emily was not amused. Not only had Tony interrupted but he was pushing Cain's buttons and Emily really wanted Cain to not think about what had happened between them before they could talk about it.

"Seriously," Tony continued talking, "the two of you need to work this shit out."

Cain growled and stuffed another cookie into Tony's mouth. "Are the Alphas ready?"

Chewing the cookie, Tony brushed crumbs off his shirt. "Yeah, Lamont wants to meet in the living room, hoping Christian will be more comfortable."

"Christian's here?" Emily asked. She had been planning on calling him later and just leaving a message. She knew he was busy but she felt like she needed to say something kind to him. Christian was a good Alpha and he had to be struggling.

Cain's eyes narrowed. Emily just peered at him, not sure how he'd changed from passionate to angry so quickly. Jeez, he was more moody than she was during her time of the month.

"Yeah, he just arrived with Adam and Kyle," Tony gladly told her, obviously noticing Cain's reaction as well.

"Cool!" She'd been friends with Kyle for years, since they were so close in age and Kyle was originally from their Pack. Although she'd never had any interest in him romantically things would have been a lot simpler if she had. Adam would have been a good choice if she'd been sexually attracted to him. He was kind and funny, but most importantly he didn't come with the same complications as Cain did. "Tell them to find me before they leave, will you?" She spoke to Tony while ignoring Cain.

Tony nodded and grabbed another cookie.

"I'll catch up. Give me a minute," Cain told his brother.

Tony glanced between the two of them and smiled before strolling away, still eating.

Cain waited until Tony had left and she could hear his footsteps going down the hall before he turned to her. "Stay away from Eric and Kyle."

"What?" she challenged. He might be dominant and the Enforcer of the Pack but he was not her Alpha or even her lover, yet. If at all.

"You heard me," he said in a dangerously low voice.

She placed her hand on her hips as her eyes narrowed. "Oh, I heard you all right. I just think you should reconsider the orders you give me."

"Really?" He walked slowly to her, his eyes never leaving hers.

"Yes," she said, lifting her chin to show she was not intimidated.

He smiled, and it wasn't a nice smile, but one of the cat before he caught and ate the mouse. He leaned in. "Okay, how's this? You'd better stay away from Eric and Kyle and anyone else I say." His eyes flashed.

Sexy, he was so sexy when he looked at her like that. Emily wondered, if she tilted her neck to him, whether he would give her a claiming bite. That was how he was acting after all. It was too bad that she had to make a stand, though. As much as she wanted Cain, she could not let him start running her life. If she did, Emily would never get the control back. "No." She said it more bravely than she felt.

"No?"

"You're not my boss. I can talk to who I want." She tilted her chin up.

He laughed. He actually laughed at her. Emily bit her lip against the whimper that wanted to escape from his touch. Be strong, she ordered herself.

"Hmm, interesting." He ran fingers lightly down her check and she shivered. "Actually, I am your boss, Emily. I am second–in-command in this Pack. A Pack where you are a member."

She pulled away. "That doesn't mean you can tell me who I can be friends with."

He'd stepped forward as she'd stepped back so he was actually closer to her than he had been before. "You don't want to push me here, Emily. Not with this."

"You're jealous," she accused. He sounded so serious and as much as she wanted to get in she couldn't. Maybe if she pointed out how he was acting he'd cool down.

"No, not jealous. Cautious." He had moved his hands up her arm and fisted one hand in her hair. He pulled gently and had her lifting up on her toes. She could have climaxed right then from the arousal coursing through her. Luckily she didn't.

"You can't keep doing this," she told him, still a little breathless.

"What?" he asked, scowling at her.

"You pull me close only to push me away again," she said. "It's not fair and you have to stop."

Some emotion she couldn't place passed quickly over his face before he straightened. "I'm sorry, I didn't mean…"

"Oh! Bullshit," she said, pointing a finger at him. "There you go again. If you didn't mean to do it, you wouldn't have done it. Jesus, Cain. I've told you that I want you. I don't know what it'll take for me to do or say to get you to believe me. That's not even the entire issue here either. You have no right to scare off anyone who might be interested in me. We weren't doing anything wrong!"

"He asked you out," Cain shouted.

"So?" Emily replied calmly. "I'm not currently attached. If you're jealous you will have to deal with it unless you're ready to admit you might just feel something for me."

"Leave it alone," he growled. "This is not the time or place to be discussing this."

"Of course it's not," she replied. "Because you didn't pick it. Well, newsflash, Cain, you don't get to decide everything in your own time."

The cool metal of the fridge against her back was a contrast to the solid heated body holding her in place.

"Do what I say, Emily, drop it." Then he kissed her quick but hard and walked away.

She was still sputtering out a response when he turned before going out of the door. Anything she might have said would have ended with her begging him to skip his meeting and fuck her against the wall. That would not help her point.

"And, Emily, you don't want to see me jealous," he called back.

There was little doubt in her mind that she just had. Replaying the last several minutes in her head, Emily was shocked that she was even still standing. Cain had kissed her, had come onto her, and it had been even better than before. He was also trying to warn her. Either from himself or what would happen if she flirted with other men.

Not that he had to worry. Emily didn't play those kinds of games. She hadn't even when he'd sent her away before. Inside the Pack, she'd had plenty of opportunity to test Cain's feelings, but she knew that was asking for trouble.

Just like she had always known that she loved him.

Cain was a great Enforcer but when it came to relationships he didn't seem to have the same communication skills. She'd known of a couple of women that he'd messed around with, heard stories while in school from her friends. One thing was for sure. Cain never slept with the same woman more than a couple of times. Emily would not be like the others. Once she had Cain, she would not be letting him go. Ever.

Chapter Four

Everyone else was already in the formal living room when Cain arrived. His Alpha sat in one of the chairs next to Christian. Kyle, Adam and Tony stood by the bar.

Tony smiled at him as he entered and Cain wanted to take his frustration out on him. Emily had really made him think last night. Hell, he hadn't gotten any sleep at all once he'd returned to the Alpha house. He'd replayed their one time together over and over in his head a hundred times. Shit, he'd even jacked off to the memory, but last night he'd looked at things from her point of view and he knew he'd messed things up.

He hadn't pressured her. Emily had come on to him because she'd wanted him just as much as he had her. She'd made the first move but when he had panicked he'd lost out on the best thing that could have ever happened to him.

With a new outlook on things, he'd been prepared to tell her how sorry he was and beg for another chance. Then he'd overheard Eric asking her out and he'd seen red, literally.

If it wasn't for his training and the control he had, Cain could have torn Eric's head from his body with one swipe of his claws.

And his wolf was close enough to the surface that he was a real threat right then. The threats against the females plus dealing with his feelings for Emily had him on the peak of just wolfing out. So what had he done? Attacked Emily and almost claimed her right there in the kitchen before acting like an ass and ordering her around. He would be surprised if she ever spoke to him again.

Fuck, he needed a drink.

He stalked to the bar and the other shifters standing there. Kyle and Adam both shook his hand, and he couldn't help but be resentful of Kyle. He was the friend to Emily that he'd always wished he could have been. Cain was aware that nothing sexual had taken place between the two but he just didn't care. Even now, looking at the young wolf with blond hair and a charming smile, Cain had to squash every instinct he had to crush Kyle's hand while shaking it.

This wasn't the time or place to let his insecurities get the better of him. He turned toward the two Alphas, everything jumping back in place. The reason for Emily's return in the first place. Christian looked tired and worn out. Cain had a job to do and that meant pushing whatever was happening with Emily away for the moment. After he accepted a drink from Tony, Cain walked over to Christian and held out his hand. Christian stood and they shook before Cain patted the Alpha on the back in sympathy. Christian had been granted Alpha status and land by Cain's father. But they had been part of the same Pack at one time, when Cain was a child. He was family to Cain and everyone else there.

Christian had only had his Pack for about thirty years, so he was a fairly young Alpha. Still, he was a good man and a great leader with a great bunch of shifters that would support him. Christian had taken a few wolves with him when he'd started out—his family and others who'd agreed to follow the new leader. Now, Christian had a girl who'd been attacked. A girl who hadn't been protected. For an Alpha to not be able to protect one of his Pack members, especially a young female, was a devastating blow. Christian was taking it hard.

Lamont got right to business, going over every detail they had learned so far and stating theories. It was a long information-sharing meeting, running over three hours. When Christian recounted what had happened to Mindy, his voice cracked. Adam went over and laid a hand on the shoulder of his Alpha, his father, but Christian shook it off. It was his burden alone to carry.

Everyone in the room except the Alphas stood and listened. They spoke no words and asked no questions. That was the way it was in a Pack—follow the Alpha, absolutely, with no questions asked.

It was decided that Cain would work with Adam, looking into the attacks and taking care of the problem when located.

Gage, another Pack Alpha, was also sending his second, Logan, to Christian's Pack for added security.

Cain did not like the idea of having to leave his territory during this mess. To leave his Alpha—and yes, Emily—without his protection, but he would have to. Hopefully working with Adam would let them catch this monster quickly and quietly.

"I think that's enough for today," Lamont stated, ending the meeting. "Christian needs to get back to his Pack."

Everyone murmured an agreement and Cain met Lamont's gaze. His Alpha wanted to speak to him privately.

"I'll walk you out," Cain offered.

Adam strode past him, followed by Christian then Kyle. No one said anything as they walked through the quiet house but Cain could understand. It had been an exhausting day.

Outside, the air was fresh and clean. Cain took a deep breath and noticed the others doing the same. With his wolf so close to the surface he would need to shift soon. The stress of the last few days was starting to get to him.

Adam slowed down, which allowed Christian and Kyle to pass them. Cain knew his friend needed to get something off his chest, so he waited.

"We find this bastard, he's mine," Adam said as he stopped a few yards from the waiting car, where they could still talk in private.

Cain nodded. If he was in Adam's shoes he would be making the same request.

"I have another favor to ask." Adam looked back at Kyle then Cain. Cain had a really bad feeling about this favor. "I am asking permission for Kyle to stay in your Pack's territory until his sister has her baby."

Kyle's sister, Alisha, had stayed with Lamont's Pack and later bonded with one of their males. They were expecting their first child and the threat could be a danger to her. Cain wanted to demand Kyle's return back to his own Pack, but he nodded, knowing it was the right thing to do. He couldn't let his personal feelings get in the way of his job. Being a fair Enforcer was important and he couldn't deny the request, since he had no reason to.

"Granted, until this is over," Cain agreed.

Adam shook his hand and nodded at Kyle. The relief that spread from the young shifter's face wrapped around Cain. He had done the right thing. Now, he just had to keep Kyle away from Emily. And it wasn't jealousy, he told himself. He was only looking out for her, like he always had. It was his job.

Kyle hugged Adam goodbye before Adam headed to the vehicle. Then Kyle joined Cain in front of the house. They both watched as Adam and Christian drove away.

"Thanks for letting me stay," Kyle said.

"No problem," Cain lied. It was a big fucking problem. "Do you need housing?"

"No, my sister has a spare room," Kyle told him.

"Good." Cain turned back toward the house. "Why don't you head over there now? I have to see Lamont."

"Sure," Kyle agreed easily. He waved then jogged to the walkway that would lead him around the Alpha house to where the other homes were located.

Cain didn't bother to watch him go. He was already formulating a plan on how to see Emily again. This time alone. As he thought, he strolled back into the house and to the study where his Alpha and brother were waiting.

They needed to finalize how to catch who was responsible and end the danger to the Packs.

* * * *

36

Cain stepped out of the shower and grabbed a towel from the hook on the wall. He quickly dried off his body before wrapping the linen around his waist. It was close to ten in the evening but this was the first time he'd had any privacy.

Cain strolled to the side of the bed and picked up his phone. He knew which cabin Emily was staying in and dialed the number by heart.

She had lived in the Alpha house like him as she'd grown up — on a different floor than Cain, but still close enough that he'd seen her all the time. When she returned from school during holidays now, she always stayed in a small guest house. It was close enough to the Alpha property that she had her privacy, but Cain also knew she was guarded well.

Still, he wished that just this once they were in the same place. He wouldn't have to orchestrate a chance meeting.

"Hello?" she answered the phone.

"I want you to meet me at eight in the basement," he told her. He was so nervous his tone was gruff and he forgot all about asking her and demanded instead. Cain closed his eyes in disbelief. He was screwing things up again.

"What for?" Her voice was cautious with a hint of annoyance.

He smiled despite himself.

He almost told her because he'd ordered her to, but he knew that wouldn't go over well. "You need to get back to training. We're not sure how long you will be here but while you are here, it won't hurt to work out. Especially with all that is going on." He wasn't used to explaining himself, but he hoped she understood that he was trying. He wanted to also put them back on the same ground.

She was so quiet he wasn't sure she was still there.

"I don't think…" she started.

No, no, no, she has to come. He needed another chance. "Eight o'clock, Emily," he ordered this time. She seemed to respond well to his dominant side. That was something he'd thought about the night before. He hoped this worked.

37

She blew out a breath and muttered something.

"I'll see you then." He hung up without another word from her. She'd be there. *God, please let her be there.*

Her words in the kitchen had really hit home. He couldn't deny the fact that he was still acting possessively over her while scaring off any other shifter male that might be interested. Luckily, she had no idea about what he'd really done years ago to warn others away from her. That would surely piss her off.

The fact remained the same, though, that every time he lost control and gave in to his desire, his need for her, Cain did then push her away.

He knew he wasn't good enough for her. Emily deserved someone who was gentle and would cater to her every yearning. Cain couldn't give that to her. He knew he was an asshole, even though he tried to be different for her. But Cain might as well be honest, at least to himself, he wasn't going to change.

Still, he couldn't continue down the same path. He did want Emily just for himself and refused to let any other shifter around her. He had to change his behavior. He'd come close to losing Emily, which at the time he'd thought was best.

It didn't matter, though. In the years that had passed, Cain's feelings hadn't gone away. Fuck no, they hadn't. He was actually more in love with her than he'd been before.

Emily was such a strong woman and anyone would be lucky to have her attention on them. Cain still worried that her teenage crush would fade away and he would be left alone, never to recover. But it was a risk he was going to have to take. Staying away from Emily didn't work, trying to push down his feelings was futile, and if he didn't get to taste her again soon Cain thought he might just go insane.

Cain dropped back onto the mattress and stared up at the ceiling. He needed to get some sleep if he was going to get up early for training with Emily.

He settled comfortably in bed before he palmed his cock.

The moment Emily had answered the phone he'd gotten hard just hearing her voice.

As he began to stroke himself, he pulled up one of his favorite memories of her.

Emily had been dressed in white shorts that showed off her toned legs. The snug red tank top she'd worn had left little to the imagination. It had been the annual Fourth of July barbeque and she'd returned home to help celebrate the holiday with her friends. Cain had managed to avoid any contact with her but as the fireworks had begun, Cain had kept his attention on her instead of the glowing night sky.

With awe in her eyes, she'd thrown her head back to watch the show.

It might have been the several beers he'd drunk that night, but the sight of Emily standing there so gorgeous and unaware of his attention had made him move closer to her. He could still almost smell the sweet scent of sun tan oil and watermelon that had drifted off her.

He'd almost reached out to touch her. Cain had even thought *to hell with everyone else.* She was too beautiful to be standing there alone.

But his senses had come back at the right moment and he'd backed off and faded into the crowd right before she'd turned around. She hadn't seen him, but he would always remember the tightness in his chest and how hard he'd been seeing her.

Cain pumped his shaft faster until he was coming. He grunted at his release. Hopefully he'd be able to fall asleep quickly. He was looking forward to beginning his seduction of Emily.

* * * *

Emily arrived tired, annoyed and mad as hell. Who the hell did he think he was? Demanding she be at the gym in the stupid morning before any sane person should be awake. This was her vacation! And he was going back to ordering her around? After what had happened the day before, he was just going to ignore it? Act like the kiss and the groping hadn't taken place? Oh hell no, she was not letting this go.

He was waiting on her, of course, standing in sweat pants and no shirt, curling weights. Her heart jumped and lust flowed through her entire body. This had to be a cruel joke. Cain was already sweating and she just wanted to drop down to her knees and yank that loose cotton down his legs. She had to get a handle on the situation.

"Who the hell do you think you're ordering me here at the butt crack of dawn to train?" she asked him with her hands on her hips. There, that sounded strong and showed her irritation.

He smiled at her in the mirror but didn't turn around. Just kept curling the dumbbell.

When he didn't answer, she took another step closer. "I'm telling you, Cain, you better stop ordering me around. I'm not going to put up with it."

He lifted an eyebrow at her. "You wouldn't have come if you didn't want to."

She fisted her hands at her sides, and he laughed. "I forgot you're not a morning person." He put the weights down and finally turned to her. "Now, would you like to stretch before we get started?" he asked sweetly.

She switched strategies. "This is not a good idea, Cain." They should just talk about what had happened. There was no way that she could wrestle around on a mat with him and act like he didn't affect her.

Cain continued to smile as he wiped the sweat off his chest. She almost moaned with the need to lick it off.

"Are you going to prepare or not?" he asked.

She didn't respond. Just turned and stomped to the other side of the gym and started stretching. He gave her fifteen minutes before walking over and nodding to the mats. She sighed, but joined him and stood in the middle. Emily bit her bottom lip as she ran her gaze up and down his body.

On the one hand, she couldn't wait to feel him against her, but on the other, this was going to be torturous. "Okay." She raised her arms. "I'm here. Now what?"

He smiled and circled her. "I think we'll start with hand-to-hand. You seem to have a problem lately with your reflexes. "

"What?"

"You've been pretty easily grabbed and touched and… mmm…kissed," he taunted.

She lifted her chin. She was a fierce competitor, and he knew it. Insults and challenges were always the way to push at her. Fine, if he wanted to play games, Emily needed to teach him a lesson. This round would go to her and when she was done showing Cain that she wasn't the same unsure young woman, she was going to get what she wanted.

"Well, don't worry. I'm wise to your tricks now so we won't have that problem again," she assured him.

He threw his head back and laughed. Then he shot a foot out at her knee and made her crumble. She fell, but rolled and was right back on her feet.

"I wasn't ready," she told him, then tried a kick of her own that he easily blocked. Emily needed to concentrate. It was obvious that Cain had kept up with his fighting while she'd been gone. She tried a roundhouse kick that he dodged. As he slipped past her, Cain slapped her ass, hard. Emily growled at him.

That started the twenty-minute battle. She landed on her ass at least a dozen times but was always right back up. She even got in half a dozen blows, one knocking him back pretty good. She finally landed a perfect jab with a kick to the back of the knee, sending him down. She yelled and clapped right before he swept her feet from under her.

He was on her immediately, sitting on her legs and holding her arms over her head. "Celebrating before your enemy is all the way out is never a good idea, Emily. I taught you better than that."

They were both breathing hard, but she smiled. "Got you down."

He looked her over with a slow, hungry gaze. "Did you? Hmm… But it looks like I finished on top now, didn't I?"

She struggled for a brief moment as he shifted his body in between her legs while still holding her arms above her head. Emily didn't really want to get away. She was more interested in making Cain work for it.

"What a very interesting position you seem to be in." He leaned in close. "Almost helpless." He licked the side of her face.

Her breath washed out of her, and she trembled with need. "Cain," she warned.

"Yes?" He moved his mouth down and licked her from her collarbone to her ear.

She couldn't help it—she moaned. "Don't. Stop."

If he needed to hear her beg she would. If he wanted to drive her crazy he was doing so. Cain could take her any way he craved as long as he finally did. He laughed softly and licked her again, this time from her ear to under her chin. She lifted her face to allow him better access.

"Which is it? Don't, or stop, or don't stop." He pressed close and teased her lips with his tongue. "Come on, Emily. Get away. Take me down." He slid his free hand down her body, teasing with light touches.

"Let go of my hands," she demanded, her voice heavy with need.

"Make me." He brushed his fingers through her clothing over her pussy, just hard enough to have her biting her lip to keep from screaming. "Make me, Emily," he said again before he took her mouth in a rough kiss.

He nibbled on her lips. She pushed up and, using his momentum from the kiss, was able to change positions briefly before she was on her back again.

"Mmm, good." He rocked against her and she could feel his erection.

"Cain," she pleaded.

He looked her in the eyes and smiled. "Oh, you'll beg before I'm done, make no mistake." He took her mouth again, and she already wanted to beg.

He released her only long enough to pull her shirt off. Before she knew she'd been released he had her hands caged once again. She struggled against his hold, desperate to feel him, but he didn't seem to notice.

"I want to touch you. Let go of my hands, Cain," she said as he continued to kiss her from the collarbone down.

"Then get your hands loose," he told her.

She struggled again, pushing up, and only managed to rub herself against the hardest part of him. For just a moment, she saw spots. She wanted — no, *needed* — him so bad.

Then, with his one free hand on her sports bra, he pulled and ripped the material. The sound of the fabric tearing was too much for her. She did beg. "Please, oh God, please."

He licked one nipple then blew on it. "Not yet," he told her, before taking the nipple in his mouth and sucking.

She screamed, but he didn't release her. He used his tongue and his teeth until she was sobbing out his name. Her body was on fire. Never had she ever been so turned on in her life. Each tug on her sensitive nub shot through her body.

"Almost there," he told her, sliding his body down to concentrate on her stomach.

He released her hands, but she kept them above her head until he pulled her pants down with his teeth. She moved quickly, pushed up and had him on his back. He let her have the position as she reached down and pulled his pants off. He was wearing nothing underneath, and she purred as she cupped his balls before stroking his cock. Then she was on her back again with his mouth on hers. He slipped a hand down and brushed a thumb over her swollen clit.

"Now, Cain. Now!" she demanded. Inside, all she could think about was getting that big hard-on deep inside her pussy — to feel him pumping his hips while holding her down. Her body was on fire and she didn't know how much more she could take before she went insane.

"You have no idea how long I've wanted to taste you," he murmured. He slipped down her body as he held her legs apart and feasted.

She screamed when he stabbed his tongue inside, using his fingers to separate her folds, then penetrating. With his thumb, he circled her clit, causing her to buck her hips while she scratched at his shoulders. Too much pleasure assaulted her. His tongue caused each sensitive nerve to dance.

"Cain!" She cried out his name as her body tightened and exploded.

"Yes, say my name," he told her as he kneeled between her legs. "Mine."

All she could do was pant in response. Her entire body was a mass of tingles and heat.

He pushed just the tip of his cock inside, then stopped. "Look at me, Emily."

When she opened her eyes, he pushed farther in.

"Say it."

"Yes." She nodded, sweat streaming down her face.

His hands held her up and in position as their gazes held. "Scream my name now."

And she did at the first thrust. Emily felt herself stretch to allow him entrance. His long, thick cock filled her like no one had ever been able to do before. It was perfect and the wetness of her first climax had him sliding easily in and out. Cain moved with smooth, strong strokes, picking up speed as he slammed into her.

Emily lifted her hips and matched each thrust, taking him deeper each time. Somewhere buried inside, she could feel her wolf start to come to the surface. With emotions so high and the fact that she hadn't shifted in too long, Emily wasn't surprised that her control was slipping.

It seemed like it wasn't only the human part of her that had wanted to be claimed by Cain. Her wolf was happily rolling over for the strong, dominant male as well.

It was unbelievably awesome to be on the same page as her animal. Having sex in the past had been more about scratching an itch. This was all about the male she was with. Her eyes had closed at some point but she forced them back open so she didn't miss a second.

Watching him, she saw his eyes start to glow and knew she was giving him pleasure. "More. Harder," she panted out.

He groaned but lifted her hips higher so he could plunge in faster, his hips snapping a quick rhythm. Sweat was dripping off his face to fall onto her chest. Emily cupped her breasts and smeared the liquid over her body. She wanted to be filled and covered in his fluids. Anything that would put his scent on her and show that she'd been thoroughly claimed.

The second release tore through her body. She arched and dug her nails into his slick skin as he reached orgasm. He stiffened right before he howled and came. His hot seed filled her pussy and she finally collapsed back.

Chapter Five

Cain rolled off Emily and they lay side by side on the mat, trying to catch their breaths. His entire body was still on fire and he was having trouble focusing on anything other than how damn good he felt.

He had no idea how long they remained on the floor until he could move again. He propped up on one elbow and looked down at her. She had a small smile on her lips with her eyes still closed. He leaned down and kissed that smile gently.

"Emily."

"Uh huh," she answered without opening her eyes.

"Emily, look at me," he told her softly.

She opened her eyes. "Cain, if you tell me that was a mistake, I think I might kill you. No, I'm pretty sure I will."

That wasn't the reaction that he'd expected, but with the way he'd acted in the past he couldn't blame her for doubting him. Instead of getting mad, he laughed softly and adjusted her where she could lie over his chest and still look at him. "No, I wasn't going to… I want you to… I mean…" He sighed and rubbed his hand over his face.

"What?"

"I want to go on a run with you. Tonight," he managed. Cain couldn't believe he was getting tongue-tied. Hopefully she would understand what he was trying to say. He watched the surprise then pleasure and, at last, uncertainty flicker in her eyes. He held his breath as he waited for her answer.

"Run?" she repeated.

He nodded. It was a big step for him. Going for a run, just

the two of them, was what mates, what bonded shifters, did. It was intimate. He wanted her to understand that she belonged to him now. To run in their other forms, their wolves, was a sign of commitment. He had to make up for the past and this was the only way he could think to show her how much he wanted to acknowledge what was happening between them.

"Just us?" Her voice was quiet.

Cain didn't know what to think about the amount of time she was taking to answer. A male could not force a female. It was up to her if she wanted to take the next step. If she said no, he had to back off, no matter what. *Please, please, please,* he silently begged for her to agree. Instead of begging, he only nodded in answer to her question.

She leaned in and whispered her answer against his lips, "Yes."

"Yes," he repeated just to hear the word again. He kissed her gently, running his hand through her hair that had come loose from its holder, trying to make up for how rough he'd just been. He couldn't stop touching her, didn't ever want to. He had fought his attraction for so long. Now, having her in his arms, he knew he would never let her go.

Hopefully she wouldn't fight him too hard. Oh, who was he kidding? Emily was probably going to put him through hell for the rest of their lives and he was going to enjoy every minute of it. He deepened the kiss and felt her shudder. "If we don't get up now, we won't make it to tonight," he told her, pulling away. Cain stood before he bent down and lifted her to her feet. It was then that he noticed the bruises on her wrists where he had held her. He stroked them with his thumbs.

"Cain."

"I hurt you." The one time he hadn't had complete control of himself and he'd hurt her. His stomach ached and he felt sick.

"No," she said, placing a hand on his cheek. "You didn't. And these will be gone in an hour. You know that," she said. Her touch was soft. Would he ever be able to offer her the same gentleness? He hoped so and would try to work at it, but he wasn't certain.

He stepped back to let her dress before he had her down on the mat again. He pulled his pants on and watched her slip into hers. She looked at the ripped sports bra, sent him an amused grin, then pulled her shirt on without it.

Her breasts stretched the material and her nipples were hard. He groaned and rubbed his chest. She was going to kill him. He picked up her ruined bra and stuffed it into his pocket before taking her hand and leading her up the steps into the main house.

He didn't drop her hand when they went into the kitchen and saw Tony sitting at the counter with a bowl of cereal, but Cain stepped in front of her and blocked her from Tony's view. It was instinct and really not needed. Tony would never hit on Emily and she would be safe with him.

Tony looked up and smiled. "Did you have a nice... workout?" he asked.

Cain felt Emily lean her forehead against his back, and he knew she was blushing. Every room in the house had extra soundproofing because shifters had such good ears, but you could hear enough. That, and Tony would be able to smell them on each other.

"Don't you have anywhere to be?" Cain snapped.

"Nope," Tony replied happily.

Cain cut him down with a look that said to be gone when he came back.

Tony just continued to smile at him. Then he sobered. "Adam called. I told him you were a little...busy and would call him back."

Emily's grip tightened on his hand, and Cain growled at his brother, who just blinked innocently at him.

"I'll call him back," Cain said then pulled Emily from the kitchen, but turned back just before the door closed and mouthed, "You're dead," to his brother.

Emily didn't say anything as they walked through the

house and out of the front door, and that worried him. He hoped she was just embarrassed and not regretting what had happened between them.

"You okay?" he asked when they reached the car she used when she was there.

Emily glanced up, appearing surprised. "Okay?" she repeated. "I'm so much better than okay."

That was a damn good answer and deserved a reward. Cain trapped her between the car and his body and dropped his lips onto hers.

He had meant it as a soft, quick goodbye kiss, but it deepened as if on its own, and his arms caged her to him. She kissed him back with the same amount of passion and need. His cock hardened and he lifted her off her feet to lean her against the side of the car. It was as though he no longer had control over his body. Cain had no idea what was happening to him and he didn't care. All that mattered was that Emily was in his arms after he'd longed for her.

The quiet, muffled sounds that Emily was making as they clawed at each other had him hard and wanting. Cain felt like if he didn't get inside her again he would go insane.

He quickly scanned the area for any others who might have been walking by or the guards making their rounds, but the area was clear for the moment. Not that it would be a big surprise to anyone to see a couple making out or even having sex.

Shifters didn't have the same hang-ups about nudity or expressing their needs for one another as humans did. The closer the full moon was, the more intense the sexual hunger grew. However, Cain could control his needs and had been doing so for a very long time. He wasn't into being watched or watching fellow Pack members get it on. He also did not want to put on a show. This was the first time that he could ever remember wanting to claim anyone in front of others, though. It was a weird feeling.

But Cain wasn't about to let anyone other than him see Emily. She was his and no one — especially another male —

had the right to gaze upon her body. That was only for him. With a growl, he trailed his mouth down her neck, nipping and sucking. He was marking his territory so that the other wolves could see and smell what was his.

Not that he thought Emily minded at all. She dug her nails into the back of his neck, holding on tight as she dropped her head back, giving him better access. Cain loved the way that Emily was responding to him. It was like her body was made for him. She moaned and rubbed herself against him, her pussy dragging along his hard cock. He lifted his head as he panted and his vision narrowed down to only her.

"Cain," she whispered sounding desperate.

"I know, baby. I know." He tried to release her but the pulse between his legs only increased when she moaned again.

He cursed and hitched her higher around his waist. Kissing her, he walked over to the trees on the north end of the property. It would keep them hidden from the house or anyone who drove up. He would hear or sense anyone else. And it wasn't like either of them really needed much time. Cain's balls were already heavy and aching. He needed to come in the worst way, and given how Emily was humping him, she might not make it until he could get her naked.

He barely had her on the ground before she was tearing his pants down. He did the same to her and plunged into her as his mouth covered her scream. Her pussy clamped around his cock, holding him tight, and he had to breathe in and out several times to keep himself from coming. As soon as he felt her start to relax, he slowly withdrew before he plunged back inside.

Heat surrounded him, and if Cain had ever felt anything that was as good then he couldn't remember. Without any thought to what could be going on around them, he thrust over and over until he was coming for the second time that day.

Cain grunted as he filled her with his seed. Emily was still clutching him when he managed to collapse at her side. He was never moving again.

"What is wrong with us?" Emily asked several minutes after they'd been fighting to get their breaths back.

Cain could only chuckle in response. He knew what his problem was — now that he'd tasted Emily there was no way that he'd ever get enough. "You're just so sexy that I couldn't resist," he told her.

She blushed, pulling her pants back on even though her hands were shaking. He reached over and grabbed them. Her confusion was obvious when her gaze met his.

"Emily?

"We just did it in the middle of the yard. Anyone could have walked by." She sounded nervous, and he smiled to reassure her.

"It's not unusual." He pulled her up to her feet with him.

She frowned at him. "No, Cain. I mean, I've been…uh…" She looked around, as if what she wanted to say would be written somewhere. "With others, you know, and it's never been like that. Well, like either time really."

She pulled her hand away and wrapped her arms around her middle. He embraced her, hoping to give her comfort.

"Baby, you haven't been with a were before, only human men. That's bound to be different. Plus, I am very good, if I say so myself. I've ruined you for all others, human or were." He was proud of that fact and might be repeating it over and over until she knew deep in her heart that no one would ever love her the way he did.

"Don't be cocky." She pushed him away, laughing. She started walking back to her car but stopped so abruptly he almost ran her over. "How do you know I've only been with humans?"

He froze. He couldn't very well tell her he knew about every one of the men she had been with. Checked them out when she'd started dating them and kept an eye out for any problems. So he told her the other truth.

"Because I put the word out if any wolf touched you I'd

51

kill them," he told her as he put his hand on her back to push her forward.

But she dug her heels in. "You did what?" Her tone was the first warning. The narrowing of her eyes the second. And her fist smashed into his face.

His head snapped back and he saw stars for a moment. When he recovered, he looked at her and saw her eyes wide with surprise.

"Ow," he complained but was also proud. Guess the lessons had paid off. Not only had she caught him off guard but she had one hell of a swing.

"You deserved that," she told him but was biting her lip.

"I did," he agreed. "Probably won't be the last either." Cain knew that he would not be easy to live with. He and Tony constantly got into fights, with them both being so dominant, but luckily for Cain, Tony was also the most level-headed shifter he knew. Tony put up with a lot from him. Even his Alpha, his dad, had given him more than one warning that Cain had better watch his mouth. Cain did not want to be Alpha, ever, but he could accidently challenge his Alpha and that would be really *really* bad.

"Probably." Emily smiled as she started back for her car.

He smiled and ran to catch up with her. "That was a good hit."

She sent him a sideways look.

"Good follow-through." He walked around her then backward in front of her. He felt young again. Happier than he had been in years. If this was what he'd been missing then Cain knew he'd been an idiot for denying her before. Well, he still thought it had been the right decision. If they had gotten together before, then Emily would have never left for school and found herself. She'd not only proved to everyone else she could take care of herself but showed herself also.

He eyed her as she strolled closer. Damn, she was beautiful. If he didn't have to return Adam's call, he would follow her back to the cabin and claim her again, and again, and again.

"Stop, Cain."

"Stop what?" he asked innocently. His cock had hardened already and he palmed himself.

Emily reached her car, but he was still in front of her. So he leaned back against the cool metal and raised an eyebrow at her while stroking through his sweats.

When he leaned in to kiss her, she pushed him back. He wasn't surprised.

"No way, or I'll never get home. You can wait until tonight."

He sent her a mournful look before tucking his hands into his pockets. And, of course, that was where her bra was. Which meant that she was completely bare under her shirt, such easy access.

"Get in the car while you can then," he warned her. Cain was really considering another round.

She laughed and went around the door he had left open. Before she could close it, he grabbed her chin and kissed her long and hard. Her eyes were unfocused when they separated.

"Drive safely," he told her as he shut the door. And he could swear he heard her growl.

Chuckling, he headed upstairs to shower. He'd never felt so light-hearted in his entire life. He was already in his room with his pants off before he remembered he needed to kill his brother and call Adam back. So he made a mental note—shower, call Adam, then kill brother. That ought to do it, he laughed to himself.

* * * *

After a short but hot shower where he barely managed not to jack off, he wrapped the towel around his waist before he picked up his cell. He dialed Adam as he sat on the mattress. "Hey, man," he greeted when Adam answered.

"Cain..." Adam sounded worn out and upset.

"What's wrong?" he asked.

"Another girl was attacked."

"When, where, who?" He jumped up and rushed to his dresser to snatch a pair of jeans. He yanked them on before grabbing a T-shirt from the drawer too. As Adam spoke, Cain dressed quickly.

"Riker's territory in Colorado. He did the same as the other Alphas and called the Pack home. Girl was fourteen miles from territory when she was attacked. She almost made it to safety."

"We need permission to go up and talk to Riker, and the girl." Cain was already making plans in his head.

"Done. Christian's already called. We leave at first light."

Cain nodded then said, "Good. Good."

"Just me and you. Riker doesn't want anyone else around the girl."

Cain frowned. "It was that bad?"

Adam sighed, and Cain could hear it clearly over the line. "Very. They don't even know if the facial tears will ever heal. Her entire body was clawed and chewed on. It's amazing she's alive."

"Fuck," Cain grunted. He wanted to rip apart the asshole who was doing this.

"Yeah, my feelings exactly," Adam agreed. "I'll be there to get you at six."

"I'll be ready," Cain promised, then hung up. He dropped his head down and took a deep breath. His stomach rolled and he felt nauseous. In his mind, he could just imagine something like that happening to Emily. She'd fight, but so had Mindy. After everything Emily had gone through as a child, she might not be able to ever recover emotionally from an attack like Mindy had suffered. Cain hadn't seen Mindy, but the way Christian spoke of her injuries made it apparent that, had she not been a shifter, she would have died.

Cain's stomach rolled and bile started to come up. He quickly calmed his breathing while gripping his knees hard.

His claws peeked out, and the bite of pain was enough for Cain to be able to regain control.

As he stood, he glanced around the room. He would prefer for Emily to stay there, where she would be closer to the Alpha and guards. He knew the cabins were safe, but that didn't mean he wouldn't worry. Maybe he'd bring it up during their run later. He pocketed his cell then headed for the door. The house was quiet but he could still sense other shifters roaming around.

It wouldn't be a bad idea to add more guards around there for his father either. As Alpha, if anyone attacked Lamont, the entire Pack would suffer. It would be a brilliant way to attempt to overpower a territory. He'd have to bring it up when he updated his Alpha.

Cain stomped down the stairs and spotted Tony coming from around the corner.

"Everything okay?" Tony asked when he saw Cain.

"Another attack," Cain answered.

"Shit!" Tony's face went from happy to angry in seconds.

"Where's the Alpha?" he asked his brother.

"His office, I think," Tony said.

Cain clamped his hand on Tony's shoulder. "Let's go tell him."

"Okay," Tony agreed. "When do you leave?"

"Six tomorrow," Cain said. "I want to add more guards around here. I have a bad feeling things are going to get worse and I don't know why yet. We need to close ranks and protect the Pack."

"I always trust your gut," Tony said.

"Lamont won't like it," Cain said.

Tony laughed. "You're right about that, but he's the Alpha and you're the Enforcer. He'll listen to you if you insist."

"Oh, I'll be insisting," Cain said. "But can you call around to some of the other Packs? I think they should be doing the same."

"I'll do it right after we talk to the Alpha," Tony assured him.

"Do you think it's weird we call our dad Alpha?" Cain questioned. He'd never really thought about it before, but with his relationship with Emily, family had been on his mind all day.

"No," Tony said while shrugging. "Our positions with the Pack allow us some distance from our dad and we need that. If we called him Alpha at the family dinner table or something that might be weird, but when talking about him as Alpha or the Pack, I think it's smart."

That was why Cain depended on Tony so much. He was not only clever, but he had the best reasoning of any shifter. Sometimes Cain felt bad that Tony was wasting all his talent with just their Pack and a small territory, but Tony appeared happy enough.

"So how's everything else going?" Tony asked, elbowing him.

"You don't want me to kick your ass, do you?" Cain retorted.

Tony snorted. "I'm happy for you."

Damn, Cain sighed but stopped right before they reached the Alpha's door. "Thanks, I'm taking her on a run tonight. It's probably been a while since she's shifted and I want our wolves to be comfortable with one another."

"You already know they are," Tony pointed out. "You've shifted together before."

"We weren't intimate at the time," Cain said. "This will be different."

"Oh yeah, it will," Tony agreed.

Cain shook his head. "I'd like her to stay in the main house while I'm gone. I'm going to talk to her about it tonight."

"Talk—not order," Tony told him.

"What?" Cain had been reaching out to knock on the door but paused with his hand still raised.

"For some reason, every time you get around Emily you turn into this giant asshole that treats her like she needs her hand held for every little thing," Tony answered.

"I do not," Cain argued. "Not every time."

"Yes, you do," Tony said. "I don't know what happened this morning but it's apparent that the two of you turned a page in your relationship. Don't fuck it up now."

Cain grunted. It's wasn't like he planned to fuck things up. It just seemed to happen when he got around Emily. "Shut up," he mumbled, then knocked on his Alpha's door.

Chapter Six

Emily nervously wiped her hands on her jeans as she waited for Cain to meet her in front of the cabin she was staying in. She liked the small house and knew if she moved back to the territory, Lamont would offer it to her. Maybe not *if* but *when*. She'd always planned on returning so that she could give something back to the Pack, but now that she was with Cain she had a decision to make. Could she really leave and chance losing Cain?

Just the thought of Cain pulling away made her chest ache. But didn't she deserve to get what she wanted? School was important to her and she didn't want to give that up either. She'd have plenty of time with Cain if he just gave her the chance. A future, maybe with their own home and kids. That was what her ultimate goal with Cain was.

That was too far in the future for her to think about now, though. First they would enjoy a run together in their shifter forms. She was both excited and edgy at the same time. For some reason this felt so much more different from any other time they'd gone on a run.

Cain had called her earlier and told her about the newest attack, but had insisted that they go ahead and shift and run. He'd told her that he needed to let his wolf out before he traveled in the morning and he still wanted to spend time with her while he could. He didn't know how long he'd be gone.

If she was being honest, Emily had expected him to cancel on her. She knew how important Cain's position in the Pack was and if he was going to investigate the attacks he had a lot to prepare. Knowing that he was making time just for her had Emily feeling special and treasured. But Cain had always gone out of his way to make sure she was taken care of. Even when he'd avoided all contact with her.

Since she hadn't had much to do that afternoon, Emily had made herself a pot of coffee before she'd sat out on the front porch of the cabin and just enjoyed the outdoors and home. The cabin was set back from the street while still overlooking the path to the Alpha house. From her view, she could see the Alpha property plus much of the territory surrounding it. The only reason she'd driven over the day before was because she'd had some gifts for Toby and some of the other young shifters. Normally she loved making the trek from the cabin to the main house.

With the gentle breeze, Emily had relaxed and thought about Cain and how she felt about him.

From the very beginning she'd felt like something was pulling her toward Cain. Now that she could look back without the taint of rejection, she remembered the way that Cain had always made her feel safe. Even as a young girl, some part of her recognized the strength and power in Cain. Emily didn't remember much about her life as a toddler and small child. Her memories before coming to the Pack were filled with being afraid and in pain. She'd never had the same feelings with Lamont's Pack or around Cain. Instead she'd felt safe and loved.

How many teenage boys would have allowed an awkward and geeky pre-teen to hang around them and follow them constantly? Cain had, and also had always made her feel welcome. He hadn't allowed the other kids to tease or harass her.

When she'd gotten older and had developed her crush on him, he'd been sweet but firm that she was too young. Even then Cain had been her protector. After he'd rejected her, Emily had wanted to hate him. She'd even told herself she did, but in truth she still loved Cain and probably always had. Knowing now that he'd warned off every other wolf both frustrated and aroused her. He'd marked his claim on her to others while remaining aloof to her. Maybe she should have hit him harder.

That thought made her smile just as Cain came strolling up the cleared path from the Alpha compound toward her cabin.

She loved watching the way he moved. Dressed only in a pair of jeans and a T-shirt, feet bare of shoes and socks, Cain appeared casual, but Emily knew that was far from how he was.

The entire time he walked, his gaze darted around and he was lifting his head and scenting the area.

Not only was Cain a great Enforcer, but he'd been trained as a guard as well. Nowadays it was Cain who put the new guards through testing before they could claim the position. Emily followed his gaze around, but she didn't see any danger. Instead, she saw the place that felt like home to her and the man who she wanted to spend the rest of her life with.

Giddy laughter bubbled up and she had to work to hold it in. So much had changed in the last twenty-four hours. She hadn't even wanted to come back because she knew she'd be running into Cain. Now she dreaded returning to school and having to leave him behind. There was no way that Cain would be able to leave the Pack, and Emily had to graduate so she could contribute to the Pack like she'd always wanted.

"Hi." Cain's voice carried to her and immediately she felt more at peace.

What was she thinking? It wasn't like Cain would just tell her their time had been nice and send her on her way. Hell, he'd already warned off the other shifters before they'd gotten together. She trusted her man to find a way to make their relationship work.

"Hello," she greeted with a kiss to his lips.

"Are you excited?" he asked but it was obvious that he already knew the answer.

"Yes!" She was bouncing on her toes. It had been too long

since she'd transformed into her wolf. She was dying to be able to run through the woods.

"Come on." He gripped her hand before tugging her after him. "I already told the guards we'd be out so nobody will bother us."

Emily grinned. She knew exactly what he was talking about. *Especially after our little performance earlier around the Alpha house.* She was blushing when Cain chuckled.

"Just relax and enjoy the run," Cain told her. "Everything else is taken care of."

The area that he was leading her to was a more private location than the main land that they shifted and ran in as a Pack. Emily was familiar with her surroundings. When she'd first begun to transform into her wolf, it had been hard for her to be around so many shifters at once, so Lamont would bring her out here. She also knew this was where Cain liked to let loose when the responsibilities of protecting the Pack got to him. Trees quickly swallowed them up as they strolled deeper into the woods toward absolute privacy. With the slight breeze, she could already feel the urge to drop down and begin the change.

Her wolf was so close to the surface.

When Emily thought of her animal, she always referred to the wolf as her wolf. As a shifter she felt the wolf inside her like a separate but very much needed part of her. She just felt more complete, like all her senses, emotions and feelings came together and she was whole.

That she belonged.

"What are you thinking so hard about?" Cain asked before he pulled her to a stop.

Emily glanced around and realized that they'd reached the small area where they would undress. A wooden trunk had been set up so they could leave their clothes and not have to worry about dirt and leaves, or other animals taking off with their belongings. "I was just thinking about how much I love to shift."

Cain nodded. "I know what you mean. I hardly ever have

to leave the territory and I don't get to change enough."

It felt good that she could talk to him about these things. "I'm almost nervous that I've forgotten how to transform," she confessed.

"Close your eyes," he said quietly.

"Why?" she asked, peering around to see if something was wrong.

"Emily," Cain added power to his voice. "Trust me."

She did, so she closed her eyes but made sure she could sense him still.

"Good," he said before he started to walk around to her back. She tried to move with him. "No," he ordered. "Stay still."

"Okay," she agreed.

She jumped when his hands came down onto her shoulders.

"Relax," he murmured against her ear. "There is no one out here but us." He started to massage her. "I can hear a rabbit not too far away — it's scurrying around, making the leaves rustle. Can you hear it?"

"Yes." She didn't even have to strain.

"The creek's close by. The water is fresh and cold," Cain told her. "The wind is picking up some of the moisture and carrying it toward us. Can you feel it?"

"Uh huh," she replied with a shiver.

Cain ran his hands down her arms. "All around us nature is settling in for the night. The woods belong to us, to our wolves. Can you shift?"

"Yes," she hissed. The muscles in her body jumped involuntarily. "Please."

When he tugged her shirt over her head, Emily raised her arms to help him.

"Keep your eyes closed," he whispered. "Let me do this for you."

Emily moaned. She would grant him anything. "Thank you."

Cain placed a soft kiss to the nape of her neck. "No, thank

you. You've always deserved to be treated so much better than you have been. I've failed you so many times."

No, what was Cain talking about? He was wonderful to her.

"Shh," he said. "I know you don't think so, but I have. From this moment on I'm committing to giving you everything you need. I want to make up for the past years where I held you at arm's length. You should have never felt alone."

And she had felt that way. When Cain had started to avoid her it had broken her heart. Still, she understood why he'd done it. She opened her mouth to assure him that she was fine with everything, but his finger touched her lip.

It was so hard to keep her eyes closed, but he'd asked her to so she did her best. Maybe it was easier for his confessions if she wasn't looking at him.

"I have no excuse except I was young, too, and thought I was doing what was best for you," Cain said. "Let me show you how special you are to me."

"Okay," she told him. *Whatever he needs to do to get us past this point.* All she wanted was her future with Cain.

"Good," he praised after she'd relaxed further. He undid her jeans and within a few minutes she was naked and barely able to contain herself.

"Cain," she said quietly. She was so close to her transformation.

"Kneel," he ordered.

She dropped to her knees with her head bent. Cain buried his fingers in her hair, and she pushed into his touch.

"Let your wolf out," he said. "Shift for me."

The rush came over her fast. Her body bent and contorted without any probing from her. She was no longer in control. Just a moment later, her vision changed and she realized she'd opened her eyes and the world around her had darkened but become sharper.

Movement from the corner of her eye had Emily turning her head in Cain's direction. He was still in human form, although he had undressed. She trotted over to him and ran her head under his palm. He petted her before rubbing behind her ears. Between the panting and soft moans, she tried to show him how wonderful his touch felt.

Finally, he patted her shoulder a couple of times before he crouched. Emily backed up and allowed him space so that he could transform and join her in wolf form.

The snaps of bones and loud crunching seemed to echo around the woods but Emily never took her gaze off him. When fur, claws and a snout replaced Cain's human form she went right over to him. She dragged her muzzle over his shoulders and sides, welcoming him as an animal.

Cain returned the rubbing and marking with scent until he'd knocked her over. Emily rolled over, exposing her belly and neck to him. She showed him that he was more dominant than she was.

Gently, he finished nosing her, accepting her submission before he sat down and gave her a low bark. Emily flopped over before she rose. He nudged her north and Emily took off.

She knew her way around and let the wolf go where she wanted. The muscles of her legs stretched and warmed and she started to sprint faster and faster. Cain was staying caught up with her behind, and, although he could pass her at any time, it seemed that he was happy to have her lead the way.

They rushed past fallen logs and branches on the way to the creek that she hadn't yet visited on this trip. The scent of the clean, fresh water was heavy in the air as she raced toward it. Emily was content to let all the worries and concerns from the previous days disappear until all she thought about was how much fun she was having.

Leaping over a large rock, she changed direction to extend the run. She didn't glance back to see if Cain followed. It wasn't like she couldn't follow his scent trail if she needed to.

A strong new smell reached her as she caught sight of

a large fox scurrying in front of her. Emily slowed down before she darted around a huge tree. She dropped to her stomach as she panted. Cain wasn't with her but she could feel him close by.

The fox stood on its hind legs as it peered around. It was a full animal and not a shifter. Emily had no intention of attacking the small thing, but the urge to hunt was strong. As if the fox sensed she was near and ready to pounce, the furry animal took off. Emily quickly went in pursuit.

Pure enjoyment went through her as she played and chased the fox around. When the little critter got tired of the game, it climbed up the tree, leaving her on the ground by herself. She glanced around trying to spot Cain. She knew he was close even if she couldn't see him. Maybe he was playing hide and seek? They used to do that all the time when they were younger and it could be a way for them to connect again. She settled down and closed her eyes so she could try to pinpoint exactly where he was.

There! She caught a snap of a branch.

Emily rose before she circled around. Cain had just stepped over a pile of leaves, no doubt trying to be quiet, but she was in perfect position for coming up behind him. He was moving and she nodded to herself. There was no doubt that he was fully aware she was stalking him. Trying to stay as quiet as she could, Emily matched him step for step. If she could use his own sound to cover hers she might just get the jump on him.

He was leading her back toward the creek and she had to pounce before they got there. The moisture in the air felt heavy and the humidity was thick but Emily was ignoring it as she prepared to get her partner. Cain paused before he glanced from side to side. She was downwind from him but with Cain's training and instincts she had to be careful. Emily waited until he turned his back once again before she launched herself at him.

Cain turned at the last moment so instead of landing on his back she knocked into his side and they went rolling.

He recovered faster than her so Emily found herself on her back with Cain standing over her while his long tongue lolled out of his mouth. He licked her snout before he ran his muzzle across her throat.

In a move as natural as anything she'd ever felt, she leaned her head back, giving him better access to her vulnerable neck. It was a wolf move—even though she kept all human reasoning in her animal form, she still had the urges of a wolf. Cain rubbed up against her, first gently, then with more pressure, marking her with his scent. Anyone close by would be able to smell that Emily belonged to him.

That thought made her so happy. Cain was letting others know that they were together. She whined and wiggled, asking for even more attention.

Cain backed up then turned his head toward the creek. She huffed before she rolled over and slowly climbed to her feet. Cain brushed up against her then took off at a careless jog.

In human form Cain had a great ass and since she was a wolf looking at another she could admit that his rear was just as mouthwatering in this form as well. Arousal started to burn inside her and all of a sudden she was in a hurry to get to the water, where they would shift.

With a bark, Emily raced after Cain.

She'd almost caught up with him when he added some speed. They both knew that he was faster so the fact that he was staying just in front of her was done on purpose.

They reached the creek and Emily stepped up to the edge and lapped at the cool water. It soothed her dry throat, the taste fresh, and she thought about jumping in. But as much as the human part of her would enjoy that, her wolf hated water. Oh, she could swim in either form but she did not like to smell like wet dog either. Not when she could get naked and sexy with Cain.

Overhead, the moon shone brightly, and she could see the reflection of her light gray fur beside Cain's nearly all black. Cain took after his father in his wolf form, although

Lamont was bigger and wider. She didn't know if that was an Alpha thing or not. Lamont was the only Alpha she'd ever met and she wanted to keep it that way. Luckily, the city was free territory and she didn't have to ask permission to study there.

Cain nudged her, drawing her attention away from her thoughts and back on him. She was doing her best not to think about him and how much she hungered for him but it seemed like Cain didn't like to be ignored.

Emily allowed Cain to crowd close to her so that she could lick him all over his face and head. She could be just as possessive and mark him with her scent too.

She could almost taste the arousal in the air between them.

Cain backed off while growling low. He was just as turned on as she was.

Cain started his transformation, and Emily followed suit. Within just a few minutes they stood across from each other, naked. Emily jumped at him, and he caught her easily before dropping them down to the damp grass beside the water. The coolness of the ground sent a shiver through her heated flesh.

"I need," she told Cain, lifting her hips so she could press against his hard-on.

"I know," Cain said. He sat back so he was kneeling between her legs and pumped his cock. "How much is the question, though."

Oh, hell. If Cain was going to tease her, Emily was certain she would go insane. "Don't…" she said. "Don't tease."

Cain's smile was wicked before he winked. "Why not?"

She groaned. "Please." Then she licked her lips, which had him tightening his hold on his cock as he stroked himself.

"Take what you desire," he told her.

Even better. Emily pushed on Cain's chest as she sat up. Cain followed directions well and soon he was lying on his back with her hovering over him. She straddled his hips, making sure she dragged her body along his. He hissed and she gave him her own wild smile. She liked being in control.

He'd released his shaft, so Emily put her hand on him like he'd done and began to pull on him. Cain gasped, lifting his hips to push into her hold.

"Now you're teasing," he complained.

"You're right," she said. In one quick, smooth move, she slid down and engulfed his cock in her mouth. His flavor burst on her tongue and she moaned. Clean, woodsy and Cain. The scent and taste were so familiar to her and her body knew it was her man. Between her legs, she grew damp and it took all her control to not jump on him instead of sucking him deep.

Her pussy throbbed as she let his shaft slip back out before she buried him deep again. She repeated the action over and over while Cain locked his fingers into her long, loose hair. She liked the same bite of pain, the tug, as she moved her head up and down.

"Stop!" Cain shouted. She lifted her head with regret. She wanted to swallow down his seed and be marked from the inside out. "I want to come inside you."

Well, that doesn't sound too bad.

Rising, she climbed back onto his lap. Cain's hands were firm on her hips as he helped her into position, until his cock brushed against her folds. She lowered down and he filled her. The heat from his shaft warmed her and it felt so damn good. This was how it was supposed to be. Her breasts felt full while the ache in her body grew.

Emily slammed back down and Cain's hands tightened on her hips while he thrust. She let her head drop back and stared up at the moon above them. *Are we all alone in the woods? In the world? It sure feels like it. Like we're the only two people in the whole wide world.* The moonlight brushed over them, Cain's eyes shone back at her, and the connection between them two of them seemed to pulse.

She lifted her hands and kneaded her breasts while riding him faster. Cain was grunting, the sound mixing with her moans. A tingle at her clit signaled her climax as it rushed over her too quickly for her to even think about slowing down.

Emily shouted her pleasure out into the wild.

Cain sat up and clamped his arms around her while plunging roughly. She panted as she collapsed against him. Cain growled, then his seed was filling her, marking her as his.

Chapter Seven

Cain pulled up in front of his home and sighed. They hadn't learned anything new from their trip to Colorado. Only that neither he nor Adam were able to catch a familiar scent on the girl's clothes. They'd been hoping, with the attack having been so recent, that something would be found. Whoever was doing this had no intention of stopping and that scared Cain. Each attack had been worse than the last and if this madman wasn't stopped he was going to kill someone.

Cain was so tired that he practically had to crawl out of his vehicle before he slowly made his way to the front door. All he wanted was a hot shower, food and some rest before he went to see Emily. His wolf was close to the surface, brought up by his frustration and need to protect. If anyone would be able to soothe the beast it would be Emily.

Walking into the house, he heard the noise and racket of numerous guests. So he probably wasn't going to get the nap. He could still get a hot shower and food, though. Cain stomped up the stairs when he caught a strong trace of a mouthwatering scent. Emily had strolled through this spot very recently. His chest seemed to throb as his wolf fought to hunt for her.

He placed his hand on the wall then shook his head. His wolf was always strong but he'd never had the feeling that his wolf was trying to break out of his body. It was a little scary, more than, but after a few deep breaths his wolf seemed to settle. He turned sharply and walked back down.

Maybe it was because their relationship was so new? He'd have to ask his Alpha. Emily had been at the front of his thoughts for the past three days and every time he remembered the run they'd shared, he grew more anxious to see her.

It had been amazing chasing her as she'd run, jumped and teased. They had lain in the woods together, just taking in the sounds of nature. He'd watched her fall asleep and had closed his eyes beside her.

His cock hardened at the memory of her taking him deep inside, riding him with the moonlight shining over her.

The words to ask to mate with her had been on the tip of his tongue when she'd dropped her head back and climaxed. The jolt that had gone through his body had sizzled him and he had rolled her over to pound himself inside her until she'd come again, screaming, taking him with her. But he feared his actions in the past might keep her from fully committing herself to him. If Emily told him 'no', that she didn't want to be with him, Cain wasn't sure he'd ever recover. That didn't mean he couldn't slowly seduce her in accepting a mate bond.

Dropping his bag at the base of the stairs, he turned then headed to look for her. She needed to join him for a shower *now*. That would take care of the first round before he hunted some food to keep up his energy for several more rounds. With a grin on his face, he pushed open the kitchen door.

Toby was in the middle of the room, tying his shoes. "You're home!" he exclaimed.

Cain smiled. That was a good greeting, and he was expecting a better one from Emily.

"Hey, champ." He ruffled his hair. "How's it going?"

Toby smiled up at him, showing a missing tooth. "Good."

"Hey, there's something different about you." Cain stroked his chin, pretending to think about it. "Did you get your hair cut?"

Toby laughed and shook his head.

"Hmm, wonder what it is."

Toby smiled, his large gap in plain view.

They both turned as the kitchen door opened. Toby scowled and bent down to finish tying his shoes. Kyle smiled when he spotted the brothers.

"Hey, just came in for some water. We got a football game in the back yard going," Kyle told them.

Toby mumbled something and jumped off the stool. That wasn't a greeting that Toby usually gave. His little brother was always welcoming to others. Cain nodded at Kyle and placed a hand on Toby's shoulder, keeping the boy from running off. Toby would tell him what was bothering him sooner or later.

"Okay, bud, let's figure this out." He studied Toby again. "It's not new shoes. Hmm, let's see…"

Toby still had the scowl on his face.

"What's up, bud?"

Toby looked down at the ground and kicked the cupboard. Cain waited patiently. When Toby appeared to finish thinking about what he wanted to say, he looked up at Cain with big eyes.

"I thought Emily was your girl," he told his older brother.

Cain nodded. "Does that bother you?"

Toby and Emily loved each other. Cain knew that for a fact. *Maybe Toby is feeling left out?*

Toby shook his head enthusiastically. "No, if she was your girl, she'd stay. Not go away again."

Cain nodded. "Okay." That wasn't actually how it worked, but Cain understood Toby's meaning.

Toby shifted from one foot to another. "But if she's your girl, how come Kyle was kissing her?"

Cain felt like he had been punched in the stomach. His vision blurred and his gums tingled like his fangs were trying to burst free. "Where?" he demanded.

Toby tilted his head at him. "On the mouth."

Cain tried to hold his fury in. He looked at the young, innocent boy in front of him. "Where were they?"

"In the living room."

Cain nodded. There had to be a reasonable explanation.

He knew Emily and Kyle, and they would never betray him. Still, it was hard to hold back a full shift. Biting his lip, he mentally pushed back at his wolf.

"I don't want her going away with him," Toby told him.

Cain wanted to gently ruffle his hair again while reassuring his younger brother, but he was afraid to touch the boy. Something was wrong. "She won't. Don't worry."

Cain kept his gaze away before he strode across the room toward the door that Kyle had just exited. A few quick words and he'd have his answer and would be able to get his control back. It would be better if Cain spoke to Kyle before tracking down Emily. Never in his life had he feared that he might hurt someone, but at the moment he was terrified of just that.

As carefully as he could, he slid open the door. He glanced down and could see the hairs on the back of his hand standing up.

What is happening to me?

"Breathe," he murmured out loud to himself. If Tony or his dad were close by, he hoped they'd be able to help, because Cain was on the verge of panic.

The warm air washed over him as he cleared the deck, but the sounds of shouting and playing assaulted his ears. It was too much. Even his heart beating was too loudly.

He smelled her, Emily, his… Cain peered across the lawn to where she was standing next to Kyle. His vision narrowed and he could only see her after a moment. Fury rolled through him and he snarled.

Emily sensed Cain, and her heart actually stuttered before resuming the steady rhythm she was used to. *How crazy is it that I know when he's near and get so excited?* When she'd heard stories of love and mating, Emily had believed they were exaggerated. Now she knew the truth.

She smiled, but as she turned, the smile immediately fell from her face. He looked furious. Had something gone wrong during his trip? Oh God, what if someone had died?

Emily wanted to offer him comfort but the rage she saw on his face had her staying right where she was. Cain appeared livid at her.

When he reached her, he grabbed her arm in an iron-tight grip and yanked her toward the house.

"Hey!" she protested but then thought better of it when Cain growled. She wasn't sure what was going on so hopefully they could get to the bottom of this mess.

He dragged her forward so hard she tripped over her own feet. She hadn't been prepared for his speed. Hell, she was fast, but there was an animalistic sense to him. Stronger than she'd ever been around. Before she had a chance to try to catch up, Cain half-turned, then picked her up and threw her over his shoulder.

Emily should have probably been humiliated, but she was frightened of him. Not for herself but for whatever had happened to cause this.

He went through the open glass door, crossed the kitchen then kicked the swinging door open into the hall. Hanging upside down, she grew a little nauseous at the manhandling.

She cursed at him quietly, demanding he put her down before she threw up. Emily could feel the bile start to rise. She started kicking and scratching when he opened the bedroom door then slammed it behind him. He dropped her on the bed none too gently.

"Cain?" Emily raised herself on her elbows. "Are you okay? What happened?"

"What the hell were you thinking, Emily?" he yelled.

The volume had her flinching away. He'd never shouted at her like that.

She blinked. "Wh…what?" she managed.

He stood in front of the bed, his eyes flashing. She could feel the shimmering in the air as he tried not to shift. Shit, what could she do to calm him? She hadn't been prepared for this. Very slowly she raised her hands in front of her. "Talk to me," she pleaded.

"Why, Emily?" Cain's voice cracked. "Why?"

"Cain, I don't know what you're talking about. Please just tell me what happened. What I did." She tried to keep her voice soft and controlled. He was pacing the room like…a caged wolf. "Cain, calm down." *Should I suggest we shift together?*

"Don't! Do not tell me to calm down, Emily. Did you think I wouldn't find out? Did you think I would just shrug it off?" His voice had gone low, dangerously low.

"Find out what?" She moved farther up the bed. She didn't like where this was going. "Talk to me, Cain."

"Shut up. Just shut the hell up," he ordered, still in that deadly tone. "What did you think I'd do, Emily?"

For the first time in her life, she was afraid of him so she kept her mouth closed — partly from fear and partly from the fact she couldn't believe he'd told her to shut up. That wasn't like him. Sure, he was domineering and arrogant, but he was never downright disrespectful.

"Answer me, damn it!"

"You told me to shut up," she blurted out. She hadn't meant to say it, but she was scared and starting to get pissed herself.

He was on her — from the door to the bed in one leap — and he sat with his knees holding her legs down and arms at her side. He wasn't hurting her, and in fact even in the yard when he'd grabbed her, his touch had been firm but gentle. That reassured her some.

"Cain." She didn't struggle. "Cain, I need you to explain to me what I did."

He snarled. "What? Do you want me to say the events step by step so you can relive your fun?"

Emily shook her head. "Cain, please…you're scaring me."

He abruptly let go of her and backed away. He curled his lip with a look of disgust.

She sat up and reached for him, but he shook his head. No, she was going to get answers. If he pushed her away she might never get him back. He loved her, she was certain, now she needed to show him she felt the same way. "Let's just talk..."

"Go," he barked.

"What?" she asked. "We need to work this out."

He turned his cold eyes at her. "Go. Get out. I don't want to see you. Don't want to be around you."

His eyes were so dark that she couldn't even see any humanity in the depths. She stood up slowly. "At least tell me why."

"Get out!" he yelled at her.

She fumbled for the door while tears ran unchecked down her cheeks as her heart broke. Cain wasn't even giving them a chance. He'd left for three days, come back mad and was telling her they were through. Years and years, they'd danced around their feelings for each other and he was saying he didn't even want to give them a chance? Had he gone crazy?

She made it out of the door and down the hall, but stopped as she ran into something solid.

"Emily." Kyle gripped her shoulders. "You okay?"

She nodded. She was numb. How could Cain turn on her? She'd been so looking forward to having him home.

"Did he hurt you?" Kyle asked her quietly.

She shook her head. Cain hadn't hurt her, not physically, but he'd also just destroyed her. The look on Cain's face was one she would never forget. She'd known he'd be home today and had hung around waiting for him. Then he'd flipped out and...

"Aww, isn't this sweet?" Cain's voice came up from behind them.

Emily jumped and slammed her back into the wall. His eyes were still the unusual black. Where was Lamont? Or Tony? They had to know what was happening. Could a shifter become possessed or something?

Kyle shifted slightly, which blocked most of her body from Cain's view. She wanted to tell Kyle that it wasn't necessary, but Cain snorted then growled.

"Coming to her rescue?" Cain spat.

Kyle looked between Cain and Emily. She shrugged but nodded to assure him that she really was okay. Kyle turned back to Cain. "Just making sure she's okay."

Cain laughed—it was sharp and angry. "Were you? Were you really?"

Cain's fist flew out and landed on Kyle's jaw, forcing Kyle through the wall. Kyle's head cracked against it and the sheet rock fell in clumps around him.

Emily screamed and ran toward Kyle to help. *What the hell!*

Cain grabbed her arm before she reached him and pushed her back into the wall. "Don't touch him," he ordered.

Emily looked up at him. He'd actually hit Kyle. Kyle was a friend of theirs. Sure, Emily was closer to him, but Cain had also hung out with him. She was sure that the noise they made would be calling to others in the house. Help would be coming. "Cain. Please tell me what's wrong."

"Wrong?" His hand snaked up to her throat. The way he'd done before when they'd been about to make love. His possession, his hold on her, marked her as his. "Why do you say something's wrong?" he murmured.

Was his voice different? Rougher? His hand tightened but still he did not hurt her. Pinned against the wall like this, she would normally be turned on, begging for him, and she actually considered it. Her body didn't know the difference between Cain claiming her and him being mad. Emily bit her lip as arousal traveled up her spine and made her flush.

"You're not laughing now, are you?" he asked. "Did you when he had his mouth on you? His hands?" he spat at her.

"He didn't touch me," she said. "No one touched me but you." Why would he even think she would betray him? If she could get him to remember their last time together, maybe he'd snap out of whatever he was going through.

He laughed. "You lie! Just couldn't wait to get another wolf between your legs." Cain moved in to cover her body with his. She was trapped between his body and the wall with his hand still around her throat.

Emily could work with this. His actions might not make any sense whatsoever, but from the way he was acting he still wanted her. He felt betrayed, like he'd been deceived. Still, he wanted her, and this was all because he had some stupid idea that she had been with Kyle.

"You know," she said. "Look into my eyes and you'll know. I've never been with any other shifter than you. In the past three days, you were all I could think about."

The hand around her neck started to shake. Cain blinked rapidly.

He was *finally* listening.

"Smell me," she urged. "I've been sleeping in your bed, alone. I have your scent on me and no one else's."

He took a deep breath. After, he lifted his head then peered down at her. If she wasn't mistaken, the color in his eyes was lightening.

"I'm yours," she told him. "And you are mine."

Cain whined, a low sound, which came from the back of his throat.

"Let her go, Cain," Lamont said from behind Cain. He looked quickly over to Kyle and watched as he tried to sit up. Cain blocked Emily from his view, and Lamont knew he had to get them separated. Whatever had happened needed to be taken care of quickly, before someone got badly hurt. He'd heard what Emily was saying to his son so he had a good idea what was going on.

The crash and shouting had not only had him coming out of his office but the others in the house had also came running. He'd sent everyone but Tony away.

Cain didn't turn, didn't acknowledge his Alpha. That was not acceptable. "Cain," Lamont said then growled. He was an Alpha for a reason and he could get Cain under control.

Finally, Cain turned his head, but still held her. He wanted to gasp at the difference in his middle boy. Cain was not in control of his wolf, although it seemed that Emily had made a breakthrough and was in the process of bringing him back. Lamont had an idea of what had caused Cain's actions and his stomach clenched in worry.

"Cain, let go of Emily," he repeated.

Cain just shook his head. His shoulders shook, his breathing rapid.

"That is an order from your Alpha," Lamont said loudly. He moved forward. "Now!" He put all his power in his tone.

Lamont watched Cain try to get control. His eyes were black, which Lamont had never seen before. As Cain blinked, they lightened.

He let go of Emily abruptly, but she immediately reached for him.

"No," Lamont said. "Both of you go to the study now," Lamont ordered.

Without looking at either of them, Cain turned, then headed down the stairs. Lamont knew Tony was standing behind him.

"Tony, help Kyle to the living room and take care of his injuries," Lamont said. He never took his eyes off Emily.

He walked slowly to her. "Come on, honey." He wrapped his arm around her and pulled her from the wall.

"Kyle never touched me. I swear," she told him softly. "Something is wrong with Cain. He would never act this way. We have to help him."

"I know, honey." He pulled her with him down the stairs.

"He didn't hurt me," she said. "As furious as he was, he never hurt me. That has to mean something, right?"

Oh God, this conversation is not going to be fun. And now that Cain was back to himself, Lamont was worried on how his son would react to his actions. "It means everything," Lamont assured her.

He led her to the study, so proud of her that she'd not only managed to calm Cain but was still trying to protect him. If he could have handpicked the perfect partner for his boy, he would want it to be Emily. He'd known for a long time that there was attraction and need between the two of them. He had stayed out of their business, trusting for them to come together when the time was right.

Now it seemed that they'd found themselves into a situation that very few shifters ever had to go through. It wouldn't be easy.

Cain had his back to them as they walked in but would be aware they had entered the room. Neither he nor Emily were being silent. Lamont gently ushered Emily to the couch before he made his way behind his desk. A reminder that he was the Alpha and in charge.

He took his seat. "Want to tell me what happened?" he asked Cain.

Cain didn't answer, hadn't faced him or Emily. That was fine for now. Lamont knew how to get through to him.

"Okay, maybe you can tell me when you two mated, and why you didn't tell your Alpha or get his permission first."

Emily's head popped up, and Cain turned. Yes, that got his attention, their attention.

"We didn't, Lamont," Emily answered.

But Lamont wasn't looking at her—he was looking at Cain.

Cain nodded. "We did not. You should know better than that."

Lamont leaned back in his chair. "And you should know better than to put your hands on a female. A girl that you swore to me that you would always protect."

Cain darted his eyes away. "I didn't mean to. I...I just couldn't stop."

Lamont looked over at Emily, who was watching Cain.

"You remember Marc?" he asked them.

They both nodded. Marc had been a young wolf, only about five years older than Emily. Marc had come home to find his female with another were and had killed them both. It was the only murder to have ever happened in his territory.

"He'd gone into a rage when he found out his mate had betrayed him. To this day, he doesn't remember what he did to them."

Emily sucked in a breath, and Cain's eyes narrowed. They could see where he was heading with his questions.

"We didn't mate," Cain told him.

Lamont believed that they hadn't intended to. But he knew, could sense, that they were indeed bonded together.

"Yet you two are very much mated."

Cain laughed. "Mated. Soul mates," he said. "Are you kidding me? That's fiction, romance novel crap."

Lamont nodded, seeing Cain had put together what he was saying. There were some things that an Alpha didn't share with his Pack. The truth of the very few fated loves was better off being considered as a myth. There were too many of them that would chase the rare gift of fated mates and would never allow themselves to fall in love and live their lives. The Alpha Council had decided that any word about the subject should be held quietly unless a couple found themselves in this situation. "It has also been said that when one mate betrays another, the pain from it can be blinding and result in things the injured mate would never normally do."

Cain shook his head. "She is not my mate."

Hurt flickered in Emily's eyes, but she quickly schooled her face.

"How'd she betray you, Cain?" Lamont asked him.

Cain turned around to the window again. He took a deep breath before looking back at his Alpha.

"She betrayed me with Kyle."

"I did not!" Emily yelled, jumping up from her seat.

Cain whirled on her. "Don't fucking lie to me. Toby saw you."

"Toby? Toby saw…" Her eyes widened and knowledge filled them.

Cain growled and took a step toward her.

"Cain," Lamont warned.

"Cain, it wasn't…" She put her hands up, but he moved his gaze away.

Emily bit her lip and looked at Lamont. "I was playing Monopoly in the living room with Toby. Tony and Kyle came in, and I—"

Cain whipped around and had her by the arms. "So you admit it!"

"No!" She shook her head. "I mean, he came in and picked me up and...kissed me for like a second. Just hello. He's been doing it for years. That's all. I swear that's all."

"That's not all!"

"Yes, it is. I haven't been alone with Kyle. Not once."

She wasn't lying. Lamont could smell it and knew that Cain could too.

"I swear, Cain." She begged for him to believe her.

He shook his head. "I just... When Toby told me Kyle kissed you, I lost it." He lowered his head. "I could feel it start to happen. I knew Kyle was in the yard. I was heading to ask him. I knew, know, that there was a reasonable explanation. I didn't really think you had but my reactions weren't mine. When I saw you... I don't really remember all of it until we were in the hall."

"I'm so sorry," she said softly.

"Don't! Don't you fucking apologize to me!" Cain's eyes burned. He could have hurt her, killed her. Lamont heard his thoughts even if they weren't said out loud. Cain turned to him. "She needs to go back to school."

Emily's gasp was audible, but Lamont wasn't surprised.

"No," he told his son.

Cain looked him in the eye. "I am asking, as your son, send her back."

"Unprotected?"

Cain frowned then rubbed his hand over his face. "No. Hell."

Emily's eyes had cleared and her voice was strong when she told them, "I don't have to be sent anywhere." She looked at Lamont. The anger burned bright. This wasn't something he could fix, though. Only Cain was going to be able to, if it was what his son wanted. "I'm going home."

She walked out without permission from her Alpha. Not that Lamont could blame her. He sighed wearily. He was starting to feel his age. Had he ever been as young and careless as these kids? Probably. His own father had warned him about arrogance. Still, Lamont thought he was a good Alpha. Cain would be too if his son had the desire to lead, which he didn't.

After she'd slammed the door, Cain looked at Lamont. "I could have killed her."

Lamont nodded. "Yes. But you didn't even hurt her. Out of your mind with rage and you managed to not cause her one ounce of pain. At least physically."

Cain flinched.

"Although I'm not sure how many times you can break her heart before she gives up on you," Lamont advised.

"I know," his son confessed. "I wanted to mate with her. I almost asked her to but didn't. She's all I ever wanted."

Lamont stood and clasped his son's shoulder. "There is no one else who suits you so well."

"I don't deserve her." Cain's voice was full of hurt. "I never did."

"So you've tried to push her away time and time again," Lamont said.

"Yes," Cain said.

"It never worked," Lamont pointed out.

"No it didn't," Cain agreed.

"What does that tell you?" Lamont asked.

"That I'm an idiot. Every time I think that I have my shit together I screw up. I hurt her and end up being an ass. She's so kind and yet I think I should have her? She needs someone who will worship her the way she deserves," Cain said.

"Why can't that be you?" Lamont asked. "You love her and she loves you. Why can't you show her how wonderful she is?"

"I don't know how," Cain confessed, pacing away. "I try…"

"Try harder," Lamont said.

Cain whirled. "How?"

Lamont shook his head. "You're not a coward. You're a good man and a strong shifter. You keep getting in your own way. Either let her go or claim her. But stop waffling. That isn't fair to either one of you."

"I need to think," Cain told him.

"No," Lamont assured his boy. "That is the last thing you need to do more of. You need to talk to your mate and beg her forgiveness. Let her calm you as you show her the love she deserves."

Cain stared at him for several minutes. The silence felt heavy around him. It wasn't something a human or even a normal shifter might feel, but an Alpha could practically taste strong emotions.

Finally, Cain smiled. "I have a mate to claim."

Chapter Eight

Emily didn't know whether she wanted to cry or to scream in anger. Fuck that, she was not going to cry, never again, over Cain, or any man. So he didn't want her around. That was fine with her, she wouldn't be around then. After everything she'd given him, he still doubted her. Well, no more. Cain was going to have to come to her this time, and if she decided to forgive him then he was going to have to get this back and forth he did about their relationship over with.

It hurt so much. But she had to stand strong. Cain had been the one who had made her grow into a strong, independent woman in the first place.

He would have to live with the woman she was. When with Cain, she had a natural feeling of wanting him to take charge and protect her. Make hard decisions. That was the old her, though.

The woman who had gone to college, made friends and decided things for herself needed to make an appearance. She wasn't a scared girl—she was a shifter, and she would not bow down any longer.

Finally, she reached her cabin and stomped up the porch stairs. She flung open the door and looked around the cabin. No one was inside so it was dark and silent. She hadn't been back to the cabin since Cain had left. It was a nice place, fully furnished. But it was also lonely. There was no Cain.

She walked to the bedroom, kicked off her shoes then climbed to the middle of the bed before curling up and thinking.

The afternoon had made one thing glaringly obvious. The bond between her and Cain was strong. They were mated together without even having had a ceremony or doing anything. Lamont had stated that they were fated to be together. Emily didn't know what to think about that. Sure, there were rumors or myths about the one person who completed a shifter being their fate but Emily had never really believed it. Now she wasn't so sure.

She could remember when she'd come to live with Lamont and the Alpha's family. She'd been scared and, even after her rescue from the cage that had been all she'd ever known, she hadn't spoken to the shifters who had saved her. They'd given her water, food, blankets and medical care. Having no choice, like she'd never had, Emily had gone where they'd told her and followed their directions. She'd learned young that it was less painful to just go along with what people more powerful wanted.

So the first time she'd seen the Pack territory, it had been through terrified eyes.

Until one brave, or maybe cocky, teenage boy had strolled up to her and bent to look her in the eye. No one else had ever done that. Normally, people darted their gaze away, but that kid had made sure she was paying attention. Then he'd made a promise.

"No one will ever hurt you again," Cain had said. "You're ours now."

She'd believed him at that moment. Hell, she still did.

Was that the moment that the fates had decided they were meant to be together? Or had she had to go through years of abuse just to end up with him and his family? It was so much to take in.

Emily didn't even know if her feelings were truly hers. Was she attracted to Cain because he was who someone or something had decided for her?

Her heart actually hurt and Emily was tired of it.

If, and God please let it be *when*, Cain got his head out of his ass and came after her they were going to set some new rules. He'd promised that she'd never be hurt again and it was time that he kept his word. No more back and forth or doubt. They were going to work this out and never visit these problems again.

Starting today, they were going to have a whole new life together.

The smart thing to do was prepare for when Cain did get there. And really, she had no doubt that he would. When she thought about what had happened earlier she didn't know whether to be happy that she could calm him when he was crazy or remain pissed off that he'd doubted her loyalty.

Emily dragged herself out of the bed before strolling toward the adjourning bathroom. She flipped on the light, her gaze catching her reflection. *Yuck!* Her makeup had smeared around her eyes, which were red-rimmed. Yes, she needed to clean up and that would go a long way to making her feel better.

The bathroom and shower had been done in a deep brown marble with large showerheads. It was pure luxury and decadence. When she had her own place or one for just herself and Cain, this bathroom was what she wanted. She turned on the water as hot as she'd be able to stand it. Carelessly, she undressed and tossed her clothes wherever they landed. As steam began to fill the room, she stepped inside the shower stall.

Heat pounded at her shoulders and she rolled them as her muscles relaxed. She placed both hands on the smooth wall of the shower and leaned her forehead against it. This was perfect for the day that she'd had. With one hand still braced, she grabbed the bar of soap with her other. Emily lathered up and started to wash. Once her body was slick, Emily went about washing her hair and scrubbing her face. She let the water wash away all the soap until she smelled just as clean as she could be.

She didn't know how long she was in the shower, but when it started to turn cold, she unhappily turned it off.

Emily pulled the towel off the hook before drying herself off. After patting her skin, she wrapped the cloth into her hair to catch the excess water. The house was still quiet but she could feel a ripple of electricity that hadn't been there before. She dressed in pajama pants and a tank top before heading for the kitchen.

She didn't turn on any lights, because she didn't need to, being a shifter. She walked slowly and made it halfway into the kitchen before she saw him. Emily was not surprised. She had suspected the minute she'd stepped out of the shower that he was somewhere close.

He sat in the chair next to the lamp, watching her. Once he saw he had her attention he flipped it on then stood. The dim light in the room highlighted the agony apparent in his features.

She didn't ask how he'd gotten in. Emily wasn't certain she'd locked the door and Cain could get in even if she had. He looked so devastated, that she had the strong urge to soothe him even if she was still hurting. "Would you like some coffee?"

He didn't answer immediately.

Emily waved toward the kitchen. "Or food?"

He stepped closer to her slowly. "Emily."

She could have stopped him. The stiffness of his shoulders told her that Cain was expecting her to. One word from her mouth, and Cain would do whatever she wanted. It was obvious that she was the one in control here. But she didn't want to punish him. He'd made a mistake, but they both knew that.

He laid his forehead on the top of her head. "I'm sorry." He lifted her chin and looked into her eyes. "I'm so very sorry."

"I know." She believed him. Even as she'd been stomping out of the office earlier she'd known. But that wasn't the issue here. Emily needed Cain to decide he wanted her and stop trying to find reasons to back off. "However, this isn't working out the way I expected. Every time I think we've finally figured things out you push me away. I can't handle that anymore."

"I'm in a new place here. I've never had these feelings before. I feel out of control…like I'm sinking," he whispered.

Emily sighed. "I understand. But, Cain, I need to know that you want me, that this thing between us is real."

"It's real," he said. "And you're the most important thing to me in the world." Cain finally pulled back to peer into her eyes. "That's what terrifies me."

"I have the same fears that you do. I've spent so much time trying to forget you and move past how much I want you. Then you give me a taste, make my dreams come true, only to shove me aside. You're making me crazy."

"It won't happen again," Cain said. "I won't hurt you again."

Deep down, Emily knew that Cain couldn't keep a promise like that, but the words were so similar to the very first he'd ever spoken to her that she simply nodded.

"I'm an asshole," Cain said. "We both know that and, really, that's not going to change. I wish I could say that I'll always put your needs above everything else but I would be lying. The Pack is important, my Alpha's needs are my responsibility, but if you give me another chance, I will love you for the rest of my life."

Emily's eyes started to water at his declaration, but she was not about to cry. Happy tears or not, she needed to prove to Cain that she could take whatever he dished out and stand strong beside him. "If I say yes we can never come back here again. It'll be you and me. We have to make decisions together. You can't go all caveman on me and make demands because you're worried about me," Emily said. "We talk things out."

"Caveman?" Cain asked with a grin.

"Oh yes," Emily said. "Me Cain, you Emily, and all the chest pounding." She laughed and the tightness in her chest popped. Happiness and excitement bubbled up.

"Okay, but if we talk and I explain to you why I need you

to do something, if it's to keep you safe, you have to listen. No more being stubborn just to prove that you can take care of yourself," Cain said.

Since she could admit that was one of her faults, she nodded.

"And everyone has to know you're mine," he declared.

Biting back a smile, she raised an eyebrow. "Am I?"

Cain narrowed his eyes at her, teasing. "Yes. Do you remember what I said to you that first day? Before I made love with you."

She nodded.

"Say it."

"Mine. You said I was yours."

He cupped her face. "That was as honest as I've ever been to myself and I couldn't hold back the words. I won't hold them back anymore either. I meant it then, and I still do. You are mine, Emily. I choose you and still want you." He kissed her gently, just a soft meeting of lips, before picking her up.

"You're mine too," she said. "We belong together."

"Let me show you how right you are." His long strides carried them into the bedroom, and she kept a tight hold on his neck.

The room that had seemed so lonely before now held such possibilities. Cain laid her gently on the bed before lying on top of her. The weight of his body pressing her down into the bed felt right. Like he was meant to be there.

She ran her hands over his back, making sure to catch the fabric of his shirt so she could touch bare skin. He leaned up enough for her to yank the material over his head. Emily placed her palm against the muscles in his chest. Her pale hand contrasted nicely with his dark, tanned tone.

"I love your body," she said while brushing over his nipple.

He shivered, and damn she loved that reaction. Emily raised her mouth to his chest and he brought his hand up to hold her there as she laved at his nipple. Then he was pulling at her tank.

She hadn't put on a bra so there was no other barrier between his hot hand and her skin. Lifting her head, she helped him get rid of the garment then went back to running her tongue across him.

The position didn't allow her to move far, so she pushed at him until he was dropping down beside her on the bed. Emily threw her leg over his and attacked the button and zipper of his jeans. She got them loose then tugged them along his legs, only to run into his boots.

"Too many clothes," she mumbled.

Cain laughed but started to lean up.

"No." She pushed him back before working at getting him completely naked. "No underwear," she said in delight before she tossed his stuff off the side of the bed.

"Now you," Cain said. "Get naked."

With her gaze on his, she knelt up on the mattress and did as he'd ordered. Once she had everything piled on the floor, Cain once again reached out. She lightly slapped his hands away. "Let me."

"Okay," he agreed as he lay back against the covers. "By all means." He waved at his body.

Now that she had him right where she wanted, Emily wasn't sure where to start. His cock stood hard away from his body and that piece of him was mouthwatering. She scooted up so she could reach him and grasped his shaft. She squeezed the base firmly then pulled.

Cain shuddered.

She did it again and again until the tip of his cock started to produce a small amount of pre-cum. Only then did she bend her head and lick at the clear liquid. The taste was bold and slightly bitter so she liked it.

With determination, she went about bobbing her head, sucking and teasing his shaft. He seemed to grow even harder under her attention.

"Em," Cain murmured. "Oh God, yes!" He pumped his hips, which drove his cock deeper and almost down her throat.

Emily choked and lifted her mouth off him.

"Sorry, sorry," he panted.

She didn't even bother to answer. She hadn't minded at all. Instead, she dropped back down then opened her mouth wider. Cain buried his hands in her hair before gently pressing in farther.

Emily hummed, encouraging him, as she slipped her hand under his ass to try to get him to thrust deeper. After several more sucks from her, he plunged out of control. She didn't pop off his shaft this time, instead she just backed off a little and let him shove himself inside. She made her lips as tight as possible while teasing her tongue against the tip.

"Fuck!" he shouted, and just when she thought he'd come he was pulling out of her mouth.

He flipped her onto her back beside him and was kissing her so fast that she wasn't able to catch her breath before his mouth was on hers.

The feel of his hard, wet cock against her thigh had her reaching for him, desperate to have him inside her. She needn't have worried.

Cain's hands bumped hers as he was also going for his shaft.

Emily moved her hands to his bare ass and let him position his cock at her pussy. She was so wet and slick that he slid in easily, filling her with one long thrust. She bowed her back, allowing him in even deeper.

Once he was buried as far as he could go, Cain hovered over her. The look on his face took her breath away.

"Are you paying attention?" he asked.

She nodded even though she wasn't. All she could think about was the way his cock was throbbing inside her.

"This is me making you mine," he said. "There is no doubts, no going back. We'll not mate officially until we have a ceremony. You deserve it. But after tonight you'll never wonder how much I love you and want you in my life."

Emily nodded. "Yes, claim me."

Cain slammed his mouth down on hers while at the same time he withdrew smoothly before plunging back in.

"Cain!" she yelled. He felt bigger than he ever had before as he drove his hips hard. *Perfect, so fucking perfect.* Emily wrapped her legs tightly around his waist, making sure to lock her ankles together as the bed started to rock.

Each time he thrust, Emily met his move. There was no slow build, no gentle touches—that would have to come later. Right then, she needed for him to be out of control and know that it was because of her.

Emily tried to hold back, she didn't want to climax so fast, but she was helpless to avoid it. She cried out her pleasure as Cain raised his head and howled his own release.

As he filled her with his seed, all she was missing was the bite of mating. They hadn't taken things that far this time, but according to Lamont they were already mated, so she knew soon it would happen.

Cain wrapped his arms around her before he rolled onto his back and laid her on his chest. She rubbed her face against his chest, knowing that her sweat would make her scent on him even stronger. When he began to stroke her hair gently, she smiled. He was just as invested as she was. The next time he forgot it, Emily was going to knock him on his ass just the way he'd taught her.

"I love you," he whispered.

She snuggled in then closed her eyes in contentment. "I love you too."

* * * *

Lamont hung up the phone with a feeling of dread.

There had been another attack. This time in Montana, more brutal, and on Pack territory. Shaking his head, he looked out of the window into the darkness.

A meeting had been called for all the Packs. It would take place in Colorado, in Riker's territory. The Alpha was still recovering himself but he'd agreed to host the other Packs. Lamont wanted to call the Alpha Council and use his contacts to get advanced information. Lamont wanted to know what the others were working on. He just didn't know if he should. Maybe starting with some of the Alphas he was close to would be better. Gage Wolf in Texas would be on top of things.

They'd been friends a long time and always were the first to send aid to one another. Yes, he'd start with other Alphas before he resorted to calling in favors.

Lamont worried what he was sending Cain into. The attacker had to know that the Packs were banding together and he would be caught soon. What if the person responsible went after the ones hunting him?

As much as he didn't want to send Cain, he didn't have a choice. This was Cain's job and what he was best at. This wasn't a good time for Cain either. Lamont didn't know how his son was faring with Emily, but he hoped that the two would work things out.

Lamont had suspected for a while now that they might be fated to mate. No two had ever fought it as hard as they had, but one couldn't miss the emotions when the two were together.

Cain had more control of his emotions than any wolf he'd known, including himself. It had been when Lamont had heard her scream on the stairs that he'd known something was wrong.

He hadn't punished Cain. Cain would be doing that to himself. Sometimes being a father was harder than being an Alpha. He had to protect them both, even if that meant protecting Cain from himself. Lamont was sure that Cain would punish himself ten times worse than Lamont would have.

He glanced at his watch. It was ten-thirty, and he didn't expect Cain back tonight. If they worked things out, Cain would be an idiot to leave her tonight. If they didn't work it out, Cain still wouldn't return. He would be off torturing himself. Lamont wanted to reach out to his son. He wanted to offer his reassurances, but he knew Cain wouldn't accept them. Cain had to figure out his own feelings.

He looked up as the knock came on the study door. Ah, he'd wondered when his eldest son would make an appearance. Cain wasn't the only one of his boys that he knew well. "Come in."

Tony walked in and nodded politely. "You got a minute?"

Nodding, Lamont gestured to the chair in front of him. Tony's timbre indicted he was talking to his Alpha, not his father. He wasn't sure how they'd gotten to where Tony spoke to him more for his position than his dad. It made Lamont sad, but he understood why Tony did it.

His oldest liked to keep his feelings and thoughts to himself. Still, Lamont knew more than Tony was aware of. He'd start trying to save Cain now. If there was anything Tony could do to protect Cain, that would be his mission. Tony's best trait was his love for his family.

Tony rubbed his hands on his pants and took a deep breath. "What are you going to do about Cain?"

Lifting his eyebrow at his son, Lamont did not answer.

"I mean. If you see fit to punish him, well, I'd understand, but…"

"Just say it, Tony."

"I should probably be punished too," Tony finished quietly.

Lamont sat back in his chair. This he hadn't been expecting. "Want to tell me why?"

Tony sighed heavily. "I knew about the first time they… were together. I was eating in the kitchen when they came up from the gym. I also knew how Cain would react to her friendship with Kyle. I didn't warn Kyle. I thought… I just wanted to give him a nudge. You know, to make a move. I don't know two more perfect…"

"Mates?" Lamont finished, and Tony nodded.

"So should I punish Toby?"

Tony's eyes widened. "No, that's not what I meant."

"Well, if I punish you for knowing Cain would be jealous of Kyle, then shouldn't I punish Toby for telling Cain about it?"

Tony would know where his father was going with this. He frowned before he sighed. "No."

Lamont nodded at him. "Honorable for you to feel guilty, but unnecessary. Cain is responsible for his own actions."

Tony nodded again. "He wouldn't have hurt her. Not like that. He doesn't have it in him. He loves her. I can feel it when he's with her."

"Yes." Lamont wasn't sure what Tony needed to hear. It seemed that the situation was affecting more than just Cain and Emily.

"I just don't understand what happened."

Lamont reached over and tried to give his son the only help he could. "I believe that Cain and Emily mated."

Tony jumped up to come to his brother's rescue. His mouth opened and closed as he sputtered out an argument. It was a crime to mate or bond without the Alpha's permission.

Lamont gestured him back down. "I don't believe they knew."

It took a moment, but the realization at what Lamont was saying came through.

"You think they were fated?"

Lamont only nodded.

Tony digested that information for a minute. "It would make sense."

They sat there for a moment.

"So what else is bothering you?" Lamont asked him.

"I don't have as much control as Cain does," Tony said.

"Very few people do," Lamont said.

"So, if Cain can lose control should I worry?" Tony asked. "Is it something in our family?"

"No," Lamont assured him. "I believe that Cain and Emily are in a very unique situation that we'll probably never see again."

"Fated mates," Tony said after a few moments. "I've read

the books you gave me. I understand why the Council wants us to keep things quiet. I can't believe we get to witness it, though."

"I've suspected for a while," Lamont said.

Tony nodded. "It will be a story that everyone will talk about."

"Your brother will hate that," Lamont said with a smile.

"Oh yeah," Tony said then laughed. "And I'll have plenty of ammo to use against him for many years to come."

"Be careful," Lamont said. "You'll fall in love too one day."

"Nah." Tony waved his hand. "I'll stay happily single. If Cain and Emily have shown me anything it's that falling in love is messy."

"And still worth it."

A wistful look crossed Tony's face quickly before his eldest managed to clear his features. "So what else is going on?"

All amusement disappeared. "There was another attack. A special meeting has been called. I have to send Cain."

Tony nodded. "He just got back today. He's with Emily right now."

"I know. I'll give him tonight with her. He'll have to be back in Colorado the day after tomorrow. I don't have a choice," Lamont said.

"Is there anything I can do?" Tony asked. "I know I'm not trained like Cain, but I want to help."

It had always been Lamont's plan to leave his Pack to Tony. His oldest had a gift that would serve the Pack well. He was a good man, all his kids were, but Tony could charm anyone. A sudden thought struck. Lamont grinned at his son. "How would you like to take the Council up on the offer to study with them?" he asked Tony.

Tony tilted his head but smiled. "You want me to accept? I thought we were going to wait."

"I'm going to call Gage, Christian and a few other Alphas, but I think now might be a good time for you to go to

California."

When the Alpha Council had offered Tony the chance to go up to their compound so Tony could learn more about heading a Pack, they'd been surprised. It had turned out that Lamont wasn't the only one who believed that Tony was going to lead a Pack in the future.

The small group of old Alphas who served as the Council to all Packs around the United States made the laws and carried out punishments. Lamont knew the other Alphas well and was proud that his son had been chosen for the great honor.

Now it seemed that he would also be able to help his Pack as well as begin to prepare Tony.

All in all, a pretty good position to be in.

"I'll phone Alpha Babcock and find out when I can go," Tony told him.

Lamont nodded. "Thank you."

Tony shrugged. "Maybe I can do a little more research into fated mates while I'm there. The book you gave me was pretty vague on what we can expect."

"I'll make sure that Cain keeps you updated as well. I don't know how much the Council is aware of the attacks, but any information you can learn will help."

"Of course," Tony agreed.

"I'll let you know what the other Alphas say at breakfast."

"Okay," Tony said. "I'm going to head to bed then. I'll call Babcock after we talk in the morning."

Chapter Nine

Emily was wrapped around him, her head cushioned on his shoulder and her hand resting on his chest, one long, slim leg thrown between his, as she slept peacefully.

He should also be asleep but he couldn't seem to stop staring at her. If he needed further proof that she was different from any of his other lovers, he realized that he'd never actually slept all night with a woman before. He hadn't even thought about not remaining in bed with her. Cain wanted to be with Emily every minute he could. Before, he'd been panicked after sex and had left as soon as he'd been able. He hadn't meant to be an ass to the women he slept with but he also hadn't wanted any attachments. For the first time, he wasn't feeling the need to run. Instead, now, he felt proud and protective. For the first time in years, the wolf inside him was so sated and tranquil that he was tempted to shift just to make sure he was still himself. Oh, he knew he was just being irrational, but how this girl had changed him was astounding. Cain was in love, with Emily, and she loved him back.

He stroked a hand down her arm to her waist. She probably needed her rest, but just watching her had him desperate to take her again. Cain leaned down and ran his tongue over the shell of her ear.

His cell phone rang and he froze like he'd been caught doing something wrong. He shook his head at his own silliness. As he strained to reach his pants, which were still hanging off the side, Emily rolled over before rubbing her face against his chest while moaning. They hadn't gotten much sleep and after the stress of the day she had to be as tired as he was.

It was six in the morning, she really wasn't a morning person in normal circumstance, and she'd been dealing with a lot. A soft whimper escaped her next. It was cute and another reminder that he would have to make sure he didn't disturb her in the future when he received late-night calls. It happened often. Something wrong with one of the guards, suspicious activity that never seemed to come to anything, or a question about the next day's schedule.

In the past, he'd accepted that it was his responsibility to be available twenty-four-seven, but maybe he needed to train one of the others to help him out.

He hated that he had to roll her off him since he couldn't actually reach the phone. Luckily, the stupid thing stopped making noise so when he pulled the covers over her shoulders and kissed her cheek she didn't stir again.

Cain climbed out of the bed, grabbing his jeans at the same time before he strolled out of the room.

His cell began ringing once again.

He took his cell phone out of his pocket and saw his dad's office number. He stiffened. Why would his father be calling him so early when he had to know Cain was with Emily?

His stomach clenched but he answered his father's call. "Hello?" he said quietly.

"Good morning, son," Lamont greeted.

"Morning," Cain replied. "What's up? Not that I mind the call but it's pretty early and I didn't get much sleep."

"I know," Lamont said. "And I'm sorry about that but I need you to pack a bag."

His breath caught. Was his dad kicking him out of the Pack? He'd known he'd messed up royally with Emily the day before but after she'd forgiven him he hadn't even thought about the punishment that would come from his Alpha. "Sir?"

"Stop thinking whatever you have in that brain of yours!" Lamont snapped.

The sharp biting tone was enough to snap Cain from his

panic. "Sorry."

"We'll deal with your situation with Emily after you return from Colorado," Lamont told him.

"I just got back from there," Cain complained. He did not want to leave Emily. No, he couldn't.

"I wish I didn't have to ask you. I'm working on some things on my end that Tony is helping me with but there has been a meeting called because of another attack," Lamont explained. "You have to be there and represent us."

"How many attacks does this make now?" Cain asked. He dropped down onto the couch. "This is stupid. We have to stop him!"

"Yes," Lamont said. "This call couldn't have come at a worse time for you but, Cain, I need you to go."

"There's more, isn't there?"

Lamont was quiet for a moment. "The girl didn't make it. She died."

"Oh God!" Cain gasped. The attacks were bad enough, but having killed a female? Fuck, he wanted to get his hands on this guy. His right hand ached and he realized that he was clenching his fist so hard that it was turning white.

"I wouldn't ask you to leave if it wasn't of the utmost importance. I know you don't want to be separated from Emily, especially now, but she'll be safest when this shifter is caught."

"I understand. I will go," Cain promised. "Emily will understand."

"That's what I thought too," Lamont agreed. "She is just as concerned about the attacks and she is going to make a great mate for you."

"We need to talk to you about that," Cain told him. Actually, first he needed to get Emily to tell him when she wanted the ceremony to take place. They had a lot of things to decide before they could move forward. She was still in school and he had a very stressful and demanding job. A position that he couldn't, and wouldn't, ever give up. But he could learn to put Emily before work, couldn't he?

"Cain, are you even listening to me?" Lamont demanded.

Fuck! If he didn't get his thoughts where they needed to be, another woman was going to be attacked or even killed. "Sorry."

"Just come up to the main house so I can fill you in. Adam is already on his way here and you need to leave in a couple of hours," Lamont said.

"On my way," Cain said before disconnecting the call. He dropped the cell onto the cushions before burying his face in his hands. Fingers gripped his shoulders.

"Shit!" He almost knocked Emily back when he jumped, not expecting her touch. "Sorry, sorry." He grabbed her wrist and pulled her onto his lap. "You okay."

"Yeah, there was another attack?" she asked him.

"Yes, and a meeting has been set up for all of us in Colorado. I have to go, Emily."

"I know."

"Emily." He held her hand tight. "I want…" He shook his head. He couldn't give her orders. "I know it didn't work out too well last time I left, but could you please stay in the main house? In my room again."

She nodded. "Of course. I liked sleeping in your bed. When you're not with me at least I can smell you on the sheets."

"And not just while I'm gone. When I get back we could move you over to stay?" He rubbed his thumb on her wrist. He felt her pulse quicken.

She smiled at him. "Are you sure? That's a big step."

He leaned over and kissed her. "Isn't this where we've been headed? Whether we mate officially or not, we're already bonded."

"I know, but we still have things we need to discuss," she said.

"You're right," he agreed. "I want it all with you. You are my future and no matter what obstacles we face, we'll work things out. Moving you into my room will allow us to be together the way I need. It'll ease my mind so I can concentrate on tracking down this fucker who is hurting people."

"I want him stopped," Emily said. "I also need you to come back to me in one piece. You might be used to going on dangerous jobs for the Pack but this isn't easy on me. If something happened to you..."

"It won't," he promised. He caught her chin in his hand. "I'm good at what I do. I have help and people I trust at my back. But you're in danger here. The attacks have moved onto other Pack territory. We've been lucky but I won't take a chance with your safety. I'll trust you to make sure you stay safe, and you can trust me to get this done and return to you."

"A partnership," she said.

"Yes," he agreed. "The two of us are stronger together."

"You're right," she said. "I'll pack a bag. I already have some stuff in your room."

"Bring it all," he told her.

"But I don't need all my stuff now. I can come back and get what I need," she told him. "You need to get to the main house and talk to Lamont."

He shook his head. "You're not returning alone. We'll take all your stuff with you so that you don't have to leave."

She sighed. "I'll bring Tony with me."

It was illogical, but he wanted to see her stuff mixed in with his before he left. He wanted that reminder that she would be there when he returned. "It will make me feel better if I knew you have everything you need."

She looked at him suspiciously. "Cain, you're not thinking about doing something stupid like locking me inside the main house, are you?"

"If I thought I could get away with it, I would." He grinned. "That's just me being honest. It wouldn't work. You'd probably tear off my balls, but it doesn't change the fact that every instinct I have is screaming at me to do just that. This is where our trust for each other will come in."

"You better help me pack then," she said, starting to

stand.

Cain tightened the arm around her waist. "Give me a kiss first."

She raised an eyebrow before leaning forward and placing a chaste kiss on his cheek.

He laughed. "Oh come on!"

"No way!" She squirmed out of his hold. "Your dad will already know what we were doing since you haven't showered. We're not having a quickie on the couch."

"Fine." He gave her the best pout he could manage.

"Yeah." She wrinkled her nose at him. "Don't do that. You look like Toby."

Cain launched up off the couch and grabbed her around the waist then tossed her up over his shoulder.

"Damn it, Cain!" she squealed, smacking him on his back. "We really don't have time for this."

Of course she was right. Who'd've thought he'd be being the irresponsible one? He strolled down the hall before reaching the bedroom. He almost groaned, seeing the bed mussed from their earlier activities. He set her on her feet just inside the room then dropped his mouth over hers and gave her a hot kiss.

She was panting when he pulled back. Cain winked before he slapped her ass. "Now pack."

"You're an evil man," she accused.

"So true," he agreed. He forced himself to walk away before he tumbled her back onto the soft mattress and claimed her again. Lamont wouldn't wait long and Cain did need to shower, pack and get something to eat before he got on the road with Adam. "I'll grab your bathroom stuff if you'll get your clothes and stuff in here."

"Okay," she said.

Cain sauntered away, his steps lighter than they should be. It would be a hard trip back to Colorado. As much as he wanted to celebrate his bonding with Emily, he had to remember that others were suffering.

As he gathered up Emily's toiletries into her cosmetic

bags, he had to wonder what the shifter responsible for the awful violence against females would be doing. Adam and Cain were certain at least that it was a male, had to be on the road constantly the way that he traveled around and showed up in different states. Was he alone or was there more than one person involved? Why or how was he choosing his victims?

There were so many questions, and Cain didn't even know where to begin to get the answers.

Normally Cain's job was to track down a guilty shifter and take him to the closest Pack or Council representative to face judgment. He almost always knew who he was tracking and why. This time he had no clue what to expect from his prey.

And this asshole was Cain's prey. Cain might have promised Adam first crack at him but Cain would stay close and make certain the shifter was punished harshly.

Once he had everything bagged up that he thought Emily would need from her bathroom, he took the items onto the bed and dropped them on top of the clothes Emily had stuffed into her duffle.

"Cain?" Emily said his name quietly.

He could hear the way her heart began to beat faster, and if he wasn't mistaken he could smell her scent begin to lace with worry. "What is it? What's wrong?"

"What's going to happen when I go back to school?" she asked.

Damn, he had been dreading this question. Since his first instinct was to tell her that she wasn't going back, he slung the bag over his shoulder, then turned on his heel and stalked out of the room. "Let's go."

"Cain, I only have one semester to go. I need to finish school."

He continued to the door. Why had she brought this up now? They'd been getting along so well and he was about to leave. He didn't want to fight with her and he knew that any conversation on this subject would result in just that.

They wanted, no, needed, two different things when it came to her education.

"We need to talk about this." She followed him through the house and out of the front door.

He didn't speak until he locked her door behind them, relieved his hands weren't shaking. Cain took a deep breath. "We do need to talk about it. It's one of the things we have to work out. But I don't have an answer for you right now." He wanted her to finish school and knew it was important to her. But that meant they would be separated from each other. He honestly didn't know if he or his wolf could handle it.

"I shouldn't have brought it up right now." She sounded so upset that he couldn't stand it. He dropped her bag before he pulled her into his arms.

"Why did you?" That wasn't what he'd meant to ask! Shit, he knew he had made a huge mistake when she stiffened and pushed him back.

"Because it was on my mind and we'd just talked about trust and being in a partnership," she told him.

"Okay," he said. "I can understand that."

She rolled her shoulders, relaxing a bit. "Well?"

"I don't know," he answered. "I can't give you an answer to that question right now and I wish I could, but what we decide will change things for us."

"So... I'm just supposed to sit back and wait for you to decide?" She huffed out a breath. "No."

"No?" he repeated, not really sure how to respond. "What?"

"I'm going back to school," she told him. "That is non-negotiable. Now that's out of the way, we need to figure out how I can do that and still be with you. We do need to have a mating ceremony as well."

"Mating..." How in the hell had he lost control of the entire conversation?

"I'd like some time to plan it, but with the semester ending soon, I'll be off for a few months. That would be the perfect time to bond officially and maybe we can even get away together," she said. Emily was pacing the front porch as she spoke. "Of course we'll have to — "

"Hold on!" He didn't mean to shout but he wasn't even sure what they were talking about anymore. "Slow down," he requested, much more calmly.

"Oh!" she laughed. "I was just thinking out loud. I don't mean to overwhelm you."

"I..." Cain glanced toward the Alpha house before peering back at her.

"Grab my bag," she told him.

With no reason not to, Cain bent down and picked up her duffle. She slipped her hand into his free one before tugging him down the steps. He felt much better once they were headed in the direction of the main house. Like he'd somehow have more of an idea how the woman he loved had gone from angry to nervous and then excited within a few minutes' time.

"I'm going to ask you some questions and all I want from you at this moment is to answer with a yes or no," she said as they walked.

"Okay," he agreed. Maybe if he kept his answers simple he could avoid upsetting her.

"Just yes or no," she repeated. "We'll work everything else out."

Hadn't he said the same thing earlier? That they'd work stuff out? Wow, this woman had him wrapped up in her spell. If there was any way to avoid this conversation he would. He had the feeling that his answers were going to be very, very important. "Go ahead with your questions."

"Do you want to officially mate with me?"

"Of course!" he said in surprise. He'd told her that.

She narrowed her eyes at him when she turned her head. "*Yes* or *no*."

"Fine," he sighed. "Yes."

"Good," she responded. "Do you want a ceremony?"

It took everything in him not to grind his teeth in

frustration. "Yes," he answered once again.

"Do you have any issue with me finishing school other than the fact that we'd be apart?"

"No." At least he didn't growl that out, although it was close.

"You have men you trust here?"

He stumbled as they crossed the lush lawn toward the Alpha house. "What?"

"Honest answer." She snapped her fingers. "Quick."

"Yes!"

Emily nodded. "Okay."

The front door opened before they'd even reached the stairs.

"You took longer than we expected. Lamont is waiting on you," Tony said as he joined them.

Cain rolled his eyes at his older brother. Tony probably thought they'd been having sex. Jeez, he could only wish. Instead he felt like he'd been put through the wringer. Not that he could tell his brother that, especially with Emily still at his side. Instead, he tossed her bag at Tony's chest. "Drop that in my room for us, please," he said. "I'm headed to the office now."

Tony smirked but he did nod just before disappearing back into the house.

Emily tugged on his hand, stopping him from crossing over the threshold. She leaned up on her tip-toes with her mouth just inches from his. "I'm going to make you some breakfast while you talk to the Alpha."

"I'd appreciate it," he said sincerely.

She brushed her lips over his. "Everything is fine here. You just go do what you need to and I'll take care of everything else."

Cain nodded.

Her smile was bright when she kissed him one last time before striding past him into the house. Cain stood just staring at the door. He had no idea what had happened but somehow it didn't worry him. He'd give Emily anything he could, so the ball seemed to be in her court. Now, he could get down to business and make sure he wasn't distracted from the task ahead.

* * * *

The drive to Colorado was long, but Cain knew when the meeting was over he had something to get home to. The sight of Emily in his robe standing at the door was one Cain would cherish during his time away. They'd showered together before he'd had to get downstairs to meet up with Adam.

She'd offered to walk him out, but Cain had just smiled and told her to stay right where she was as he grabbed his bag.

The robe had been way too big for her so she'd attempted to wrap and clench it closed, but the opening had gapped and her breasts had just been barely visible. Even thinking about it right then, he was hard.

He shifted in his seat, trying to get comfortable and calm down before Adam noticed anything. Not only would his friend be able to see his hard-on pressing against his jeans, but he'd also be able to smell his arousal. And that would be embarrassing. He glanced over at Adam and frowned.

Adam had been silent for most of the trip. They had stopped for coffee fifteen miles back and Cain had taken over the driving, but Adam still wasn't sharing what was wrong.

The strong emotions coming off him smelled a bit like desperation and anxiety. He'd expect a little of both, but these were just too potent. Something else other than this case was bothering him. If anyone could get answers out of Adam it would be him. He was not about to let his buddy suffer alone. He'd help Adam figure out whatever the problem was. He also had a good idea where to start. He'd bet Adam just needed someone to listen to him without the worry of putting the Pack in danger.

A troubled or weak Alpha put the entire community in danger. Adam was keeping his concerns close to his chest, but Cain would offer whatever assistance he could. They both knew that Cain had no interest in becoming an Alpha and being in charge of an entire Pack.

"How's your dad doing?" Cain asked.

Adam sighed.

"Adam?" Cain pressed.

"Still depressed and blaming himself. He won't listen to me, to anyone, that it wasn't his fault," he finally said.

"Other Alphas, other territories..."

"I think what happened to Mindy reminded him of something in his past. He's having nightmares and he'll lock himself in his room," Adam said.

"Oh jeez," Cain blurted out. He hadn't realized things were so bad for Adam and Christian. He'd been so wrapped up in his own drama that he'd let down the people who were like family to him.

He and Adam had been raised together, as Christian had served as his father's Beta. When Christian had been given his own Pack it had broken both his and Adam's hearts to be separated. Sure, they understood why, but it hadn't been easy to let go of that closeness.

"I should have been there for you." Cain felt guilty.

"Nothing you can do," Adam assured him.

"No, I could have..."

"Left your mate alone and come keep an eye on me and my dad," Adam finished for him.

"No!" Cain argued. "Just been more available, I guess."

"Cain, I know if I call you day or night you're going to answer. If I'd asked you to come down, you would have been there. It just wouldn't have helped."

"So what can I do now?" he asked.

Adam shook his head. "Nothing. You spent some time in Texas with Gage Wolf's Pack, right?"

"Yeah." Cain nodded as he glanced in the rear-view mirror before putting on his blinker. Their exit was coming up, and he changed lanes before giving his attention back to Adam. "Dad and Gage have been friends for years. That Pack is awesome."

"My father and Logan grew up together," Adam said. "He's there now with him."

"Logan's been staying at your house?" Cain asked.

"Yeah," Adam said. "I'm hoping with me being gone, Logan can reach him. They seemed to have an understanding that I just don't get. Whatever is wrong, it seems that Logan knows exactly what the problem is. I think he's just trying to come up with the solution."

"If anyone can it would be that guy. Especially if they're as good friends as you've said. That guy is fucking brilliant," Cain said.

"I like him," Adam said. "I just feel...comfortable around him."

"It's what makes him such a great Beta. Your dad does the same to me. They are just so calming to be around," Cain agreed.

"Usually," Adam said. "Not so much more anymore. My dad is so full of... I don't even know how to explain it."

"You don't have to," Cain told him. "Just vent, let it out, I won't judge you, your father or anyone. Nothing you say will ever leave this car."

Adam stared out of the window. "He wants me to take over the Pack."

Cain jerked the wheel in surprise. He quickly corrected his steering before he realized he'd almost missed his exit. He slowed and followed the other traffic off the highway until they turned onto a much less traveled road.

"That was pretty much the reaction I had." Adam laughed bitterly. "Except, luckily, I wasn't in a moving vehicle, although I did drop a crystal glass."

"You'd be a good Alpha." Cain wanted to make sure that his friend knew he believed in him.

Adam finally looked at him. "Do you think so?"

Cain didn't hesitate with his answer. "Yes, I do. I guess

it just shocked me. Your dad's still in his prime. He could lead the Pack for several more years. Lots more years."

"That's what I told him," Adam said. "He said he's lost the taste for it."

Suddenly Cain was assaulted with an overwhelming sense of fear. "Adam! What is it?"

"I'm worried that when Logan leaves, Dad might want to end his existence."

"Fuck." Cain swerved again. He immediately hit the knob for his blinker before he started to pull over to the right, out of the way of traffic. He could not continue this conversation while trying to drive.

Once the vehicle was on the side of the road with the hazards flashing, Cain turned to his friend.

Cain knew shifters who had done that. Ended their lives or had someone do it for them. It wasn't common, but it had happened in the past enough times that Cain had been trained in the symptoms to look out for in case one of his Pack members was in danger.

"Maybe he won't," Cain offered, not knowing what else to say.

"I guess we'll find out soon. Logan got word that his Alpha is expecting his first child. He'll need to return to guard over them. Gage won't want anyone else near Marissa. He's overly protective on an average day, but this is going to send him spiraling out of control."

Cain smiled. Marissa Boyd and Gage were having a baby. That was awesome news. He was glad to hear that Marissa was still happy in her new home. Gage's mate was one of the few weres who couldn't shift and had recently come across her old Pack that had abused her terribly. Marissa had ended up changing a lot of people's beliefs on non-shifters.

Thinking of Gage having a child made him think of Emily. She would be a great mother. The way she was with Toby was proof of that.

It was something they needed to discuss. He could picture

their children running around playing while he held her in his arms. Not right away, but he actually wanted to think about it.

Emily was changing him, for the better, and Cain hoped he wouldn't screw things up completely.

Just as things were coming together for him, his best friend's life was falling apart. Cain wanted to help but he wasn't sure what he could do. Adam was a smart, kind and strong man and he would be a great Alpha, but Cain hadn't thought his father was doing so badly.

"What can I do to help?" Cain asked.

Adam looked over at him. "Actually, just talking this out with you is helping," Adam said. "I'm just so overwhelmed."

Cain nodded. "So let's break it out. Here." He reached into the glove box for a notebook and pen. "Take this and write down what needs to be done. The Beta is helping you?"

"Yes," Adam said. "Luckily our Pack isn't as big as yours, so everyone is doing what they can to help each other, but this isn't how it is supposed to go. Our family should be taking care of business so the rest of the Pack can enjoy their lives and not worry. We're never going to be able to help Mindy and move on if the Alpha and inner circle are falling apart."

"So do it," Cain said.

"What?"

"Your dad wants you to take over the Pack because he is unable to handle it right now for whatever reason. He might recover or could get worse, but this isn't just about him. It sounds to me like you want to fix things, *so do it*," Cain said.

"I can't help him," Adam said. "So maybe I can do something good for the rest of the Pack."

Cain patted him on the shoulder. "Exactly."

"It's not as easy as it sounds," Adam told him. "I've been running things for several weeks now but things I need his decisions on aren't getting done."

"Then decide," Cain told him.

"I can't!" Adam threw up his hands. "I'm not the Alpha even if he wants me to be. The Council would have to approve the transfer and that takes time."

"You're thinking too much. You need to make sure the Pack is running well, help Mindy and protect everyone. Just make those decisions that are needed and get things happening. If your dad wants the Pack again he can take back over, and at least no one else will be hurt. If he formally requests retirement than you already have things set up the way you want," Cain advised.

"I'm worried that he'll think he's not needed. There's no telling what he'll do then," Adam said.

Cain understood what the issue really was. Adam was capable, but he was holding back out of fear that his dad would end his existence knowing the Pack was safe. He had no idea how he would feel if this were happening to him. "Adam, you need to do your best for the Pack. Your father is a great man and while he's struggling now, that won't last. He'll get past this and everything will work out."

"I hope so," Adam said. "You're right, though, I do need to step up."

"Good." Cain straightened so he could get them back on the road. "Now let's talk about this meeting."

Adam sighed. "Yeah, even that has to be better than everything going on in my head."

Cain flipped on the turn signal to return them to the highway. Once traffic was clear, he pulled out. "I'm not sure how I feel about Riker." The Colorado Alpha was not a nice guy. He was often too harsh with his Pack, and Cain didn't like that.

"I don't like him," Adam told him. "My dad says that he's very old-school and believes that all Pack members have to fight to get high positions. He pits them against each other so there's a lack of trust and closeness. It's a good thing his Pack is smaller, like mine. Can you imagine if he had as many members as yours?"

"It wouldn't be good," Cain agreed. "Do you think he's involved in this? He didn't appear very sympathetic when it was one of his own Pack."

"We went around the entire property searching for the scent of the attackers. Wouldn't we have picked up on something?" Adam asked.

"Yeah," Cain said. "You have a point."

"Of course that doesn't mean he didn't set it up," Adam added. "If he used someone outside his Pack, maybe even a rogue. He did get our attention and now one of the largest gatherings of all the Packs is on his territory."

"I asked Lamont why we were meeting there and he wasn't sure whose suggestion it was, but I can imagine Riker insisted. The others would agree just to get it over and done with. We've got to catch this guy."

"It could be dangerous," Adam said. "If he is involved and we're all on his land."

"He can't make a move against all of us. Our Alphas would hunt him down, but I do agree that we need to be careful. I don't trust him," Cain said.

"After the meeting, I'd like to sniff around," Adam told him.

"Okay," Cain replied. "I'll see what I can do to cover for you. Just don't get caught."

Adam scoffed. "Come on, I was taught by the best."

"I am the best," Cain said smugly. He laughed as Adam grinned.

It might have only been something small, but at least Adam had a smile on his face. If Cain had a chance, he'd get a hold of Tony and see what his brother could do to help. Tony was heading to California to the Council property, but Tony always had time for him. He'd also make sure that his brother kept what was going on with Adam's father under wraps for now. He didn't want the Council to get involved yet. Christian could still pull through.

"Thanks," Adam told him quietly.

Cain only nodded. No other words needed to be said

between the two friends.

* * * *

The moment he walked into the meeting, Cain knew that it wasn't like the others he had attended before. That in itself wasn't a shock, since the assembly had been arranged as a result of such horrible violence. What was troubling him was the way the different Packs' representatives were all edgy and looking at each other with suspicion. If they turned on one another they wouldn't get anything done.

As he and Adam strolled closer to the large conference table, he dipped his head respectfully at the other shifters in the room. Riker wasn't there yet and as far as Cain knew he would be the only Alpha attending.

It was unusual for Alphas to leave their territory, especially during a time in which they were needed to protect their Pack. He spotted Sam, Gage Wolf's third-in-command, and sat next to him.

"Sam," he greeted his friend quietly.

"Hey, Cain, Adam," Sam returned with a nod. "Glad to see you both here." Sam glanced around the room and the smell of unease was flooding off him.

Sam was a guard who had recently been promoted and spent most of his time looking after the Alpha mate of his Pack, Marissa. Cain didn't think Sam had ever attended a summit for the Packs. But with Logan off territory it would fall on Sam to attend and report back to Gage.

Cain clamped his hand down on Sam's shoulder and squeezed. He leaned closer and in a low voice said, "Just stay calm and don't get involved in other Packs' business," Cain advised. "Sit back and listen, pay attention to the others, but don't bring their interest to you."

Sam nodded before he relaxed. "Thanks."

"Sure," Cain said. "I've been there. I remember my first summit by myself."

"I hope it was under better circumstances," Sam

whispered.

"It was," Cain told him. "But I was still scared shitless I would disrespect the wrong wolf and start a Pack war."

"Yeah," Sam said. "Gage already has enough on his plate and I don't want to add to it."

"Don't worry, Adam and I have your back. Everything will be okay."

The room filled up quickly, and finally Riker walked in. He went directly to the head of the table and sat. Since he was the highest rank, he would run the summit.

There were nine territories being represented but twelve seats taken. While Riker was representing his own Pack, he would also be allowed to have one of his men at his side to help run the meeting but also look out for their interests. Larry had walked in behind Riker. Cain didn't know much about Larry. He would have had to fight well to be so high in the Pack, but Cain didn't know anything about his personality. The fact that Larry belonged to Riker's Pack at all made Cain suspicious of him. An Alpha could tell dominance inside a wolf without the need for violence. Cain didn't respect a bully and that was how he thought about the entire Riker Pack. This was only one of the reasons that Riker's reputation was that of running an old-school Pack. Wolves were used to violence, and Riker seemed to encourage it.

In the last two chairs sat two shifters that Cain didn't know, but he could feel their power. Both men were built and extremely intimidating, even to him. One had dark brown hair and to the left of him was a slightly smaller light-haired guy. They had to be the representatives from the Council, and Cain was happy to see them there.

Cain's doubt and unease about Riker was still bothering him, and the only ones present who would be able to question or take on the Alpha without causing issues for their home Pack would be the Council guys.

"Let's get this summit started," Riker said. "First, I'll go over what we know, then we'll open with suggestions on how to catch the person responsible for the attacks. We need to outline what all of you are doing in your own territories to keep the members safe and where you are investigating. There is no point in duplicating research when we can better spend our time elsewhere."

Cain leaned back as he listened to Riker update everyone.

The survivors had all given the same description. The attacker was out to cause as much pain and humiliation as possible. After he sexually attacked the girls, he would beat them with his fists. The beatings had rapidly gotten worse until the last victim hadn't lived through it.

Cain peered around, taking in the reactions of the others, until he met Larry's gaze. Cain took an immediate dislike to the man. There was no compassion in Larry's eyes as Riker spoke about the results of Mindy's attack. Adam was gripping the edge of the table and his fingers were turning white. Not moving his eyes, Cain leaned against Adam so to offer him some comfort without anyone else picking up on it.

He would have liked to excuse Adam from this part, but that would show weakness that the Packs couldn't afford. Adam took a deep breath before releasing his hold then leaning back.

Larry was still staring back at him.

Sam shifted beside him, and Cain noticed he was also staring at Larry. Sam tilted his head, and Cain got the impression he was scenting him. Larry's attention went to Sam before he sneered. Larry had obviously picked up on what Sam was doing as well, but instead of appearing irate he sent them a smirk.

Sam sat back in his chair as if nothing was up. Cain had to give Sam credit. Larry was more dominant than the younger guard, but if he was scared or worried he wasn't giving off any vibes like that.

It was taking all his control not to wipe that expression off Larry's face, so he looked back at Riker and began to pay better attention to what the Alpha was saying. Cain wasn't about to share what little they'd been able to find out. He didn't know who was involved and if they had a connection to anyone in the room. It became obvious that several of the others felt the same way when Riker asked for updates and no one spoke up.

"We need to work together," Riker stated loudly.

"With respect, sir," Sam said beside him, "maybe if you start, it'll help pave the way."

Cain could have fallen out of his seat at Sam. It was one thing to suspect an Alpha or Pack but to openly ask wasn't something he would have done. Damn, maybe he had underestimated the young guard.

Riker glared at Sam then peered around the room as if he was daring anyone to agree with him. Cain was about to do just that when the light-haired stranger stood.

"My name is Clint Price and I am one of the Alpha Council representatives. This is my partner Kurt Moore. We're here to ensure cooperation between the Packs and to assist in any way possible in locating the suspect. We don't work solely for the Council but were tasked to them temporarily from our own Packs. This means we want to find this monster and get home. So you are going to share information so we can hunt this asshole down."

Clint took the time to meet each shifter's eye at the table before he sat back down.

"What if we don't have anything to share?" a female shifter asked.

Cain glanced over at her. He didn't recognize her.

"You're Ginger Winters?" Kurt questioned.

"Yes, my brother is the Alpha of the territory closest to this one. We're concerned about our own Pack but we don't know anything and from what I understand no one else does either."

Kurt nodded. "Which is the purpose of this summit. So the Packs that don't have all the information about the attacks can go back to their territory and make sure they are protected." He glanced around the table. "But some of you are investigating."

Cain sighed. He wasn't going to give away everything Lamont had updated him with that morning but he could give them something so maybe someone else would share. "Right now, we're looking into rogue shifters that were kicked out of their Packs and might have exhibited behavior that matches the attacks."

Several people leaned forward.

"Have you got any leads?" Kurt asked.

"No." Cain shook his head. "But it's somewhere to start. It's hard to believe that this guy has never done something like this before. The attacks are so violent but he's not leaving evidence behind. He either knows what he's doing or he has learned from his mistakes in the past. This can't be the first time he's attacked someone or had the urge. He might be escalating from wherever or whatever he's done before but if we look close enough there has to be a connection."

Kurt nodded. "I agree."

"I have the sheriff looking at arrests of sexual assaults of this nature also," Larry spoke up.

Cain snapped his head to Larry, surprised.

"He's human, so I can't tell him why, but he owes the Pack some favors so he'll get what he can," Larry added.

That was smart. Cain didn't know if his Alpha was doing the same, but it was worth bringing up.

"We were also looking at rogues," an older, weathered-looking man said. "Someone who had approached different Packs trying to get in. My Alpha is working with the other Alphas on this. We think he's targeting Pack members from specific territories."

Cain finally recognized the older shifter from a small Pack in Oklahoma.

That seemed to have opened up communication as talk finally got underway with ideas and suggestions on how to find the suspect.

* * * *

Adam got his chance to shift at the end of the meeting when he excused himself to go to the restroom. When Adam caught his eye, Cain knew his friend was making his move.

"We're about done here," Cain said loudly enough that those around him would hear. That way they wouldn't question Adam not returning.

It was hard to keep his mind off what Adam was doing while the others stood and spoke their goodbyes. He did keep his gaze on Riker and Larry, though. He didn't want either one of them catching Adam.

Sam seemed to slip away and Cain saw a red-headed woman approaching.

"Ginger." She offered her hand.

"Cain," he greeted, shaking her hand, but then released her quickly. "Your Pack is close?"

"Yes." She smiled. "We're smaller than most of the others but we like it that way." She dropped her eyes and looked him up and down.

He could pick up the attraction and if he didn't have Emily he would have been tempted to take her up on the offer she was giving him with her body language. She leaned closer before trailing her finger over his shoulder. "Are you staying here? Maybe we could get together later?"

He smiled. "A week ago, I would have been more than happy to, but I'm with someone."

She stuck out her pretty bottom lip but nodded. "I can't change your mind? A week isn't that long to have made a lifelong commitment." As she shifted on her feet, her breasts rubbed against his chest.

"I have to get home to my mate," he told her. "It's new, so we haven't been together long, but it is that serious."

Ginger laughed. "Well, it figures. A good-looking guy like you can't be single. Sorry I hit on you. I didn't see a mark."

"It's okay," Cain assured her. "We'll be having a ceremony soon."

She had backed off, giving him the proper distance, and he was glad she didn't push it. Ginger was a beautiful woman, but Emily was the only one he wanted. The only one he had ever wanted.

"I better go," Ginger said then sent him another beautiful smile. "But good luck with your mate. And congratulations!"

"Thank you." He grinned as she walked away.

The room had almost cleared out completely. Only the two Council representatives, Riker and Larry, remained. He sauntered out of the room and toward where he'd parked. He hoped Adam was about done running around because they didn't have much time.

The front door was open so he strolled through and began to search for Adam. His friend was leaning up against the car talking with Sam.

Cain spotted Brent Simpson and waved. He hadn't gotten to talk to Brent at the meeting but it appeared Brent was in a hurry as he quickly returned the wave but continued getting into his SUV. He'd only met the man once, when Cain had made his first and only trip to New Mexico. Brent had been the one to show him around, and although Cain wouldn't say they were friends, Brent was a nice enough guy. Cain would have liked to pull him aside and see if he had any information that he hadn't shared.

With the urgency of getting all the intel back to their Packs, Cain could understand why Brent was in a hurry.

As he reached Adam and Sam, he could hear them talking about Adam's little side visit. Obviously Sam had picked up on what they were up to.

"Anything?" he asked Adam.

"I didn't pick up the scent of the attacker anywhere around or close to the house. I don't think he's a member here," Adam said. "Or at least staying here."

"Damn." Cain ran his hand over his face. He was tired and if they didn't get a lead quickly someone else might be hurt or killed. "We need to end this fast." He glanced over at Sam. "Did you get anything from scenting Larry?"

Sam smiled but shook his head. "No. There is something about him, though. Although there was a strange scent in there and I at first thought it was coming from him. But I couldn't locate it. It was like it was some kind of cologne."

"What kind of smell?" Adam asked.

"Just a sharp pine and sweet scent. It was weird," Sam said.

Cain had to agree. He'd smelt the same strange scent but hadn't thought anything about it at the time. Most shifters didn't wear any type of perfume or fragrance since they had such strong noses. Still, it wasn't unheard of.

"So someone could have been trying to hide their scent? The attacker, maybe?"

"Son of a bitch." Adam growled. "And we let him go?"

Cain put his hand on Adam's shoulder to calm him. "We don't know that it was. But it gives us an idea. We do know who was at the meeting, and that gives us a place to start."

Adam shrugged off his hand. His eyes brightened. Cain grabbed the back of his neck. "Relax, Adam, this is good news. We'll get him."

"Before he goes for the next girl?" Adam snapped.

Sam moved restlessly, and Cain knew he could tell how close Adam was to shifting. "Yes, if he is here he's not out stalking his next victim," he told his old friend.

"You're right." Adam took several deep breaths before nodding. "Sorry."

Sam slapped him on the back. "Had me worried there for a second. Well, I've got to run. I want to call Gage and fill him in."

"Tell him we said hi," Cain told him. "Oh, and congratulations on the baby!"

"Baby," Sam said with a shake of his head. "I had no idea how Marissa getting pregnant was going to affect *me*. She's driving Gage crazy with all her cravings, so in turn he's driving me crazy, sending me after things. I have instructions to stop on my way home and pick up a list a mile long. I tell you, I don't think I want children after seeing this."

Cain laughed and slapped Sam on the shoulder before strolling to the driver side of the car. "You okay?" he asked Adam.

"Yeah," Adam said while opening the passenger door. "I just want to get this guy. Let's get on the road so we can make our own phone calls."

Sounded like a plan to him. The sooner they left, the sooner he'd be back with Emily in his arms.

The meeting hadn't been as much of a waste of time as he'd expected it would be. The Packs that had been directly involved were all working hard to discover who was responsible and now they had better organization. He actually felt like they were finally making progress.

He started his vehicle before putting it in gear. As he began to pull out of the drive, he spotted Larry and Riker walking out of the front door. Cain still didn't like either man but at least they were trying to find the attackers. Or they had at least provided some ideas.

Larry glanced up as they drove past.

Cain didn't look away as his gaze once again met Larry's. He still had an uneasy feeling about the guy. To him, anyone who rose up as far as Larry had in Riker's Pack had to have some bad in him. To fight for dominance was something that almost no shifter did anymore. It seemed like the members in Riker's Pack thrived in that environment, though.

There was already so much pain in the world. Cain wanted to make it where none of his fellow Pack members ever had to witness it. Cain and Larry held the same positions in their Packs, but Cain was relieved that he was nothing like the other shifter.

He might be an asshole, but Cain truly loved his family and those he was charged with taking care of. There was no way he'd be worth Emily's love if he was the kind of Enforcer that beat others to show his strength.

Emily deserved to be cherished and loved. Cain was going to have to make sure she got all that and more. And he knew that she deserved to finish school and be able to contribute to the Pack using her education like she'd always wanted.

That meant he would either have to let her go back to campus alone or work out a way to split his time between her and their home. Since he couldn't even imagine only seeing her every few months, Cain was figuring a way to work things out. He'd already decided to give some of his top guards more responsibility, but maybe he needed to do more.

Lamont would support whatever decision he made, so he didn't have to worry about his Alpha being upset. Still, as soon as they caught the attacker, Emily would need to return to campus, and Cain was going with her. She had one more semester and it would start in a few short weeks.

Of course, if they didn't catch this guy then Emily would have to stay longer. Maybe put off returning to school until the next year. No, he couldn't allow that. If he found anything to lead them to a suspect he would get the guy. If there was another attack and he could have prevented it he would never forgive himself. He would have to take Emily back to the apartment and her classes. No matter how tempted he was to keep her away from everyone else in the world.

Chapter Ten

Emily ran around the large tree in the middle of the Pack's running grounds and pulled her shirt over her head. She had long ago learned not to be shy about her naked body, but she didn't think that Cain would much like his brother seeing her that way. Actually, as jealous as Cain had acted the last time he'd returned, she knew for a fact he wouldn't like it. She'd been restless all day waiting for Cain to get home. She didn't like being away from him. It also made her realize that she couldn't go back to school with him staying inside the territory.

Sure, she'd told him that she wanted to go back to campus and meant it, but she hadn't understood how uneasy she'd feel when he wasn't close. Emily wanted to be with him all the time. She'd never felt this way before, which made sense, since she was supposedly mated to Cain. It had taken all her control not to call him and stay on the phone until he pulled up in front of the house. She'd needed a distraction.

Tony had suggested she should take a good long run to calm herself. He should have already left for California but Cain had called right after his meeting asking for his brother to stay until Cain could update him.

Emily hoped that meant they had a lead and that soon this monster would be caught.

As she pushed her jeans down her hips, she heard the sounds of Tony's shift. She needed to get out of her own thoughts and hurry up and change forms.

The wolf inside was scratching to get out, making her clumsy as she undressed. After folding her clothes and placing them against the trunk of the tree, she kneeled and welcomed the magic that would allow her to shift. The tingling started at the tip of her toes and moved over her body quickly. Her skin grew tight, until it felt like it would burst. Bones adjusted inside her, and she felt herself float like she always did.

Then, only minutes later, she stood on all fours, tilted her head back and yowled in pleasure. An answering call from the west told her that Tony was ready. She bounded for him, content to run and play until her man came home to her.

Tony wasn't as large as Cain and his fur had red streaks over his shoulders. Her animal knew him just as well as she did Cain, but the feelings that Cain brought to the surface were much more different. Tony felt familiar, as a brother would.

Family, love, peace—those feelings flooded her as she rubbed her head under Tony's chin. She didn't like that he was going away. Even if it was to fulfill his dream of working with the Council. He'd told her all about his assignment over lunch. While she was happy for him, she was going to miss the calming influence he had on the Pack, her and Cain.

With Tony gone, Cain would be needed even more at his father's side. If she asked him to go with her he wouldn't. *Couldn't.* Cain's devotion to the Pack was one of the things that she loved most about him. Her need to finish her education was going to tear them apart. Unless she gave up her dream.

Tony nudged her, and Emily understood that he wanted to get the run started. She looked up and was surprised to see sadness in his eyes.

He was leaving. He wouldn't be able to run in his own territory. While she was celebrating being home and getting to feel the soil under her feet, Tony was saying goodbye for a while. She had no idea how long he would be gone—if it was going to be a week, a month or longer.

Emily pawed his side then took off running as fast as she

could. They weren't on the same path that she'd taken with Cain but instead where the majority of the Pack ran. It had been so long since she'd been in that part of the woods that it took her a little while before she could orient herself.

She leaped and rolled, enjoying the feeling of being carefree and happy in her shifted form. One plus of staying in the territory instead of returning to school was being able to shift whenever she wanted.

In the city there was just no safe place for her to shift. Their existence was a secret for the protection of all the shifters in the world. She couldn't risk someone seeing her, or worse, getting a picture or video. The increase in technology was not a shifter's friend. Everyone carried a smart phone nowadays and just one leaked photo could put them all in danger. So Emily had never changed away from home.

As she'd stayed away from the territory for longer and longer, she'd gotten used to not transforming, but it had never felt comfortable.

It was a choice to transform. She might feel the pull of the moon because of nature and her animal, but there was no truth to the 'weres changing at the full moon' myth. She could shift when and where she wanted to. Except for times of extreme stress, most shifters remained in control of their animal.

Times like this where she got to let the wolf run wild were just so fantastic.

Beside her, Tony was keeping pace, and if his happy face was anything to go by he was having as much of a good time as she was. It was just the two of them out there, as it was the middle of the day and most of the Pack were at work or were busy. It was like they had the entire woods just for themselves.

They ran another mile before Tony paused, blocking her path. Emily looked around, confused. It couldn't be time to head back yet. Cain wouldn't be home for another couple of hours.

Tony batted his head against her side until she lowered herself to the ground. He stood over her with his ears twitching. Emily tried to calm herself so she could concentrate. The run had taken a lot out of her and she was panting. As she breathed, she sniffed the air.

There was a faint scent of someone she didn't recognize. The person had been right where she was lying not too long ago. She jumped to her feet in alarm. Tony immediately pushed her back down.

Okay, he was too strong to fight, and he needed to stay alert. He was keeping his gaze in the direction of where it seemed the scent had disappeared to.

She whined softly. What were they going to do? Lamont and a couple of guards knew where they were, but there was no telling how long it would take before they realized they hadn't returned. Plus, she didn't know what the strange scent meant.

Another shifter would know by Lamont's markings that this was Pack territory and they shouldn't be there.

A ripple of energy emerged beside her, signaling that Tony was shifting. Once he was crouched down in human form, real fear enveloped her. Tony wouldn't shift like this if it wasn't one hundred percent needed.

"I want you to start heading back toward our clothes. One of the guards should be close to that spot to keep an eye out for us," he said.

Emily nodded.

"I will be right behind you but I want to make sure no one is following," he added.

Again, she nodded. It wasn't like she could argue as a wolf. She whimpered even though she wanted to be strong. Lamont had told her about what had happened to Mindy and she was scared.

"Hey," he said, rubbing his hand over the top of her head. "You're going to be fine. I won't let anything happen to you."

She licked his other hand.

129

"Okay." He patted her one last time. "Let's go."

Emily waited until he had changed back into a wolf before she started off in a fast lope. She moved quickly but was also having to be aware of her surroundings. Now that she remembered the area better, she took the most direct route.

She glanced several times over her shoulder to make sure Tony was there. She couldn't see or hear him but she just knew that he was there.

Up ahead, she could see where she'd stashed her clothes. Emily jumped over a thick tree root then stumbled to a stop as a large wolf darted in front of her.

Emily sniffed but she didn't recognize this male.

Growling, she tried to sound as menacing as she could. The strange shifter growled back before he launched himself in her direction.

* * * *

After dropping Adam off, Cain drove faster than the speed limit. He couldn't shake the feeling that something wasn't right. Picking up his cell phone from the middle console, he tried once again to reach Emily.

It rang four times before he got her voicemail. Dread filled his stomach as he tried his brother. No answer there either. He'd spoken to both only a couple of hours ago but now Cain wished he had insisted that Emily be inside the main house until he got there. Not knowing where she was and if she was safe made him feel like he couldn't breathe.

Cain stomped his foot harder on the accelerator, and the car shot forward. Tony had been waiting on him to get there, and Emily had promised to not go anywhere alone. They should be answering their fucking phones.

He dialed Emily's number again before tossing the phone on the passenger seat in disgust. Cain took the next turn too sharply and the car skidded. Correcting the vehicle, he took a deep breath and slowed down. Getting himself killed wasn't going to help either of them.

His cell phone rang from where he'd thrown it, causing him to swerve again in surprise. The number of the main house showed on the I.D.

"Emily!" he answered.

"No, it's your father. What's wrong, Cain? I can feel your unease from here." His father's voice was soft but sharp, pulling him out of his panic.

Cain laughed almost hysterically. Why hadn't he thought of calling the house? Of course his father could sense when he was worried, so why wouldn't he be able to sense if Tony was in trouble?

"Cain, are you okay?" his father asked again.

"Yes. Yes, I'm fine. I couldn't get a hold of Emily or Tony, and I started to freak out. I didn't even think of calling you," he tried to explain.

His father's sigh of relief was audible even over the phone. "Emily and Tony are both fine. She was so restless waiting on your return that they went for a run."

That made Cain feel better, but he just wanted to be absolutely sure she was okay. "Can you sense them?"

When his father remained silent, Cain knew he was trying.

"Yes. Emily is very happy right now, and I believe she is outrunning your brother."

Cain could picture Emily in her small limber wolf body running from the bigger black wolf. While his brother was big and powerful, Emily was smaller and faster. She had almost outrun Cain the first time they'd gone out.

"Thanks. I'm only about thirty minutes away, but I could feel something wasn't right." He still had that feeling, but it had lessened. He still felt on edge, just that something wasn't right.

"It's probably just your bond. You've been away from her for too long. I'll have Kyle go tell them you're almost here."

Cain felt a growl try to escape from the back of his throat at the mention of Kyle.

"Cain." His name came out as a warning.

He shook his head to clear his mind. "That would be

great. I'll see you soon."

He drove like a madman and actually made it in just under twenty minutes.

Cain pulled up to the gates and waved to the guard to open up. Antonio waved back as he pressed the button to let him in. Cain looked in his rear-view mirror, still uneasy.

The drive to the house seemed to take hours even though it was actually less than a few minutes. He had his seat belt off before the car came to a complete stop.

Lifting his head to the wind, he concentrated on the sounds and smells around him. Then, using the mating bond, he tried to find Emily.

He could sense her behind the house, still in wolf form. She was only about a mile away. He started to go to the house until another smell reached him. One mixed with hers. He knew that smell. It had been at the meeting. The unusual mixture of pine and sweetness.

Cain took off running while pulling at his clothes. He shifted as he ran, which was as painful as it could get. Once on his four feet, he could run faster. That didn't stop the black and grey wolf coming up from behind and passing him. His Alpha. *So Lamont could sense the trouble too.*

He sped up and ran after his father into the woods. His ears picked out a loud growl then a whimper. He ran faster, jumping over fallen branches instinctively as he headed in the direction of Emily.

When he and his father broke through to where the sound of battle was already taking place, he immediately sought Emily.

His brother, in wolf form, was fighting a larger wolf while another went from snapping at the strange wolf to blocking Emily from it.

Lamont howled and headed into the fight. The strange wolf threw Cain's brother off his back and met his father. The sound of impact when Lamont threw himself at the stranger echoed around them.

Cain ran to Emily to make sure she was okay. She seemed

unharmed. Her small frame was hunched down but there was no blood. There were little whimpers coming from her and that did worry him. The wolf guarding her moved aside as Cain approached. Looking in his eyes and smelling him, Cain knew who he was. But if Larry was the wolf protecting Emily, who was his father now fighting? The only reason Larry and the stranger had beaten him there was because he'd had to drop Adam off, but that shouldn't have given them that much of a head start. If Cain wasn't sure that Larry had been protecting Emily he would have his fangs buried in Larry's throat.

Cain nuzzled Emily's neck and could have cried himself when she used her small tongue licked his paw. She knew he was there and everything would be okay. He shifted away from her and nodded at Larry. Thankfully Larry understood and moved to stand guard in front of her once again. Next, Cain checked on his brother, who was lying on his side, panting. Tony was injured but alive. He turned to the dark wolf who now stood muzzle to muzzle with his Alpha.

Lamont darted in and nipped at the dark wolf, making his opponent have to scramble around. Cain waited patiently while Lamont distracted him until the perfect moment. Then he jumped, knocking the dark wolf off its feet, causing him to stumble. The dark wolf tried to regain his footing, but Cain pounced and held him down.

They rolled, teeth clashing, as they both tried to get the upper hand. Distantly, Cain could hear Emily's whines and his father taking care of Tony, but he couldn't look back and give up his attention on the attacker.

The wolf made a move to get his back legs under Cain. It was just what he had been waiting for. Adjusting his body weight, Cain got a hold of the wolf's neck. He slammed him down hard once, then again. His sharp canines sank further into the fur until the attacker gave up.

Going limp, he submitted to Cain.

Cain remained on alert as other members of his Pack—

both in wolf and human forms—joined them. It was Antonio who spoke quietly to Cain, telling him to release his grip. But the wolf inside Cain wouldn't let him. Instinct told him to rip the wolf's throat out for endangering his mate. Then his father was there in human form, adding his voice to Antonio's. But it wasn't until Emily dropped next to him, human and naked, and placed her hand on his head that he could. She was back in human form and he could smell her fear and relief.

The betrayal he felt was keeping him from being able to think clearly. He knew the wolf that he held by his powerful jaws.

This wasn't some stranger that had just happened to cross paths with their Pack or Emily. The attack against his mate wasn't random.

Cain growled and shook his head again just so he could hear his captured prey's pain. He couldn't believe this was even happening.

"Cain." Emily stroked his shoulders.

That was what he needed to make the final push at his instincts so he could release his foe. Letting go of the wolf, Cain crawled into her lap and started his own shift back, staring into her eyes the entire time. It hurt—the adrenaline in his body was so strong that he had to force the transformation.

Once he was back in human form, Emily began to cry and he pulled her into his arms as she shivered and wept. He couldn't believe how close he'd come to losing her.

"Is she okay?" Antonio asked as he placed a jacket over her.

Cain hadn't even realized she was still naked. He tried to help her get the jacket to cover her body but his hands were trembling. Another pair of hands assisted Emily when he could not. Not only was his body fighting to recover but he could also not believe that the attacker was Brent Simpson. *Brent Simpson... what the fuck*?

A man who he knew had been the one responsible for

those atrocious attacks on the females. Had he always been evil? When Cain had met him had Brent already had this planned? He'd been so sure a rogue would have been involved in the crimes.

He turned and glared at the other non-Pack member present.

"You knew," he accused Larry. "You followed him here and didn't tell us!"

"I had my suspicions," Larry told him, shrugging. "I wasn't sure, so I decided to follow him when we left the meeting. There was no reason other than to hide his scent to bathe in that smell. I didn't know where he was going so I had nothing to tell anyone. By the time I figured out his destination, I couldn't call since I needed to keep him in sight."

Cain was still shaking with rage at the thought of any man putting his hands on his mate. Even though he knew Larry had helped protect Emily, she wouldn't have needed that protection if Larry had given him a heads-up.

Emily's soft hand turned his head toward her. "He saved me, Cain. I was trying to make my way back to my clothes when the other wolf appeared in front of me."

Cain tightened his hold on her.

"He came out of nowhere. One minute he was standing in front of me, and the next, he attacked. Tony tried to get to me but this guy was there faster and he held him off until Tony arrived. I don't know what would have happened if he hadn't…"

"Shh…" Cain ran one hand over the back of her hair, letting the silk fall through his fingers.

"No, I want to tell you," she insisted.

Cain nodded, knowing she needed to get out what had happened.

"He had me pinned down, and I really thought he was going to kill me. Then, all of a sudden, he was gone. Larry had pulled him off me, and they started fighting. Then Tony ran in and joined the fight." Tears welled up in her eyes.

"It's okay," Cain said. "I know he saved you. I just have to calm down."

"I'm so sorry, Cain. I just wanted to run."

"Oh, baby, it's not your fault." Cain let her bury her head in his chest as she cried. He looked up and met Larry's gaze.

"Thank you." It wasn't enough. It would never be enough to him. But this man, who he had suspected of being involved in the attacks, had saved his mate's life.

Larry shrugged and half-smiled. "I'm just happy that Brent has been caught and we can all move on and begin to heal."

"Why not tell your Alpha?" Lamont asked, walking up and handing Cain Emily's clothes.

Larry barked out a laugh. "Things run a little differently in my Pack. If Riker had come into what you had, he would have watched the fight and then offered the winner a job."

"Sounds like you need a new Alpha," Cain commented.

The shadow that crossed Larry's face was brief, but Cain had seen it. He wondered if maybe Larry wasn't as happy in his position as Cain had believed.

"Maybe I do," he whispered softly. He looked around the area surrounded with Cain's family and friends, his face showing a bit of longing. Then he backed away until he blended in with the trees and was gone.

Cain didn't stop him and his father only watched him go. They couldn't really do anything to keep him there and he probably hadn't gotten permission from Riker to be gone.

Still, Cain now owed Larry. He hoped he could find a way to help him get away from Riker, if that was what Larry wanted. Cain would come up with a plan.

* * * *

"Cain?" Emily rolled over and reached for him as she called out his name. The bed beside her was empty. She sat up and saw him sitting on the end of the bed. "Cain?" She moved up behind him and wrapped her arms around his neck, pressing her breasts into his back. He hadn't said much once they'd gotten back inside the main house.

He'd been so gentle with her as he'd led her to his bathroom and into the shower. He'd washed her with soft strokes until all of the day's activities had seemed to run down the drain with the water.

Knowing he needed time to process, she hadn't pressed him to talk. Instead, she'd taken his hand and they'd fallen into bed, where they'd held each other tight. It seemed he was taking what had happened even harder than she was. But she hadn't been hurt, at all, and she needed him to overcome the attempted attack. "What's wrong?"

"What's wrong?" He laughed bitterly. "You could have been killed yesterday while I wasn't even here."

Emily sighed and crawled onto his lap. "I could have been killed even if you had been here."

He shook his head. "He knew I was with Adam and he could beat me here. He went after you because you're my mate."

Emily understood. "And you blame yourself."

"Of course I do." Guilt laced his words. "He heard me telling someone we were going to mate so he decided to go for you!"

She placed her hands on either side of his face and made him look at her. "You love me." When he started to respond, she put her fingers over his lips. "You love me, and you're afraid that because of that I'll get hurt."

When he didn't deny it, Emily knew she was right. "But here's another thing. I love you too. I love you so much that when you're gone, I find myself going crazy thinking about you." She placed a soft kiss against his lips as she moved her hand. "There's always going to be danger, Cain. Whether I'm with you or not. I'd rather know that you'll always be looking out for me than have you push me away because of it."

"That's just it, though. I'm so selfish that I would rather have you in danger than give you up."

Emily smiled, hoping he would understand. "I need to be with you, Cain. Always. I don't want you to ever give me up."

He visibly relaxed and under her bottom his cock started to come to life. She wiggled and nipped his bottom lip. "Seems to me someone is feeling better," she said as she teased him. She didn't think she'd ever get tired of the way he responded so quickly for her. It was heady knowing that she was the reason he walked around with a hard-on.

With strong hands, he cupped her ass and pulled her tighter against him. They hadn't dressed after the shower earlier so his shaft slid against her clit.

"I'll show you just what I'm feeling." And he kissed her.

Emily had never known a kiss to be so sweet and promising in her whole life. He drugged her with his caresses and tenderness. She wrapped her arms around his neck before burying her hand in his hair so she could hold on tight.

Cain broke away, and she tried to follow, not wanting to lose his taste yet.

"One more thing," Cain said, his lips brushing hers.

"Enough talk," she demanded, reaching to fist his hard cock.

"Just have to tell you this…" he panted as she started to stroke him.

"What?" she asked impatiently. Why did Cain want to talk at that exact moment? She was already wet and desperate to have him. She needed to show him that she was okay and had to have him inside her soon. She rubbed the tip of his cock with her thumb, trying to get him on the same page as her.

"I'm going to talk to my father and promote Antonio to Enforcer so he can take the out-of-town jobs," Cain told her.

Emily stilled her hand. Had she heard that right? "You're staying here with me permanently." Joy filled her at the thought of not having to be separated from him again. This last trip had been hard and she'd already decided that she just couldn't be away from him. Knowing he felt the same way and was making changes for her meant so much.

"Well, no."

Emily's heart jumped in her chest. "No? But you just said you wouldn't give me up." If Cain started his back and forth bullshit again, Emily was going to absolutely knock him flat on his ass.

He looked at her for a full minute before a smile broke out on his face. "I'm not."

"But...I don't understand," she said, trying to slide off his lap so she could follow the conversation better.

Cain tightened his hold on her hips, which was almost as distracting as his cock against her.

"I'm going back to school with you. You'll finish the semester and then we'll return here together. To our home," Cain said.

"Cain!" Emily didn't know what to say. On the one hand, she was getting what she wanted but, on the other, he was giving up everything for her, and she couldn't allow that. "I can't let you do that. You love your job. To give up your position..."

"I'm not giving up anything," he told her. "I'll split my duties with others but I will still work with the Pack. There is a lot I can do over the computer and phone. Plus, I was hoping you'd be able to pick your classes to have Fridays off so we can come home on the weekends. Whatever we need to do to stay together. It's only for a little while."

She hadn't expected Cain to want to do this for her. At that moment, she truly believed that he was ready to commit fully to her. She'd been so frustrated with how he'd changed his mind and seemed unsure, but he'd finally proven to her his willingness to make sacrifices. "Thank you."

I would do anything for you, honey. And this is just a small thing. You want to finish school, so I want to support you. When you're done, we'll return here and continue our lives together. Have a couple pups when we're ready to support the Pack."

Once again, tears fell down her face. Her dreams were

coming true. After the horrific events that had been happening, she had something to be grateful for in the end.

"No crying! This is a good thing," he complained.

Emily scrubbed the tears from her face with the back of her hand. "Happy tears, Cain. You've made me so happy!"

"I'll always try to make you happy. But, when we return, I will take my post back as the main Enforcer for the territory. When we come back on the weekends, I'll have training schedules to oversee for the guards. Are you okay with that?"

"Yes! Yes! I know that's who you are. I understand that!"

"Okay then, enough talk."

She squealed as he flipped their positions so she was on her hands and knees on the bed with his body over her. His cock was still hard as he pushed against her. She wanted him to take her exactly like that. Emily dropped her shoulders to the mattress and wiggled her ass. "Take me, claim me as your mate."

"Are you sure you don't want to wait for a ceremony?" he asked. "I want to do right by you."

Fuck! Why couldn't he just take her at her word? She didn't want to stop and have another heart to heart. For someone who hated to talk, Cain sure was killing her. "I don't need that," she told him. "All I wanted was you and I got that."

"Yes, you did," Cain said, sliding deep inside with one smooth thrust.

Emily clenched her inner muscles around his shaft while curling her fingers into the sheets. He withdrew slowly before he plunged in again. Sensations ran rampant through her body as each stroke took her higher and Cain began to pound her hard. The grip he had on her hips was going to leave marks, but that only turned her on even more. They might have technically already been mated but she wanted it to be a conscious decision they made together. "Bite me."

"You'll always belong to me. You will be under my control," he told her, thrusting faster.

"Okay. Yeah." She would agree to anything.

"Just like I'll be yours and I'll only give up my control to you."

Emily slammed back into him. "Yessss..." she hissed. She felt his canines against her neck. He nipped her skin but didn't bite. "Yes," she said again.

He pierced her skin as she screamed out his name and her body exploded. He pumped his cock deeper and harder, until he was coming along with her.

Emily's arms shook and she lowered herself down with Cain's big body still on top. With her face buried in the pillow and her bones feeling like they'd been melted, she didn't ever want to get up. This was the most perfect moment that she could ever imagine.

When Cain started to separate from her, she gave a little whimper, not wanting to lose his heat and weight.

"Let me get something to clean us up with, then we'll take a nap," Cain told her. "I'll be right back."

It was hard since she was so comfortable but she managed to turn her head and watch as he padded across the room to the bathroom. His fine ass flexed as he walked, and she loved the view. She heard the water in the sink being turned on briefly then off before he reappeared in the doorway.

He stopped when he saw she was looking at him. "See something you like?" he teased.

"No," she told him. "Something I love."

Cain laughed. "That's sappy, but I love it and you too. But don't expect me to start talking like that. I'm still the same asshole I've always been."

Emily propped her chin up on his hand. "Oh, I absolutely believe that. But you're sweet too."

He snorted but strolled toward her. When he reached her, he used the warm washcloth to clean her before he tossed it over his shoulder. "If you tell anyone that I might have to gag you."

She smiled up at him. "Don't worry. I wouldn't want your reputation to suffer. If anyone asks I'll still tell them you're a complete bastard."

"Good." Cain nodded. He climbed back onto the mattress before he pulled her up until her head rested on his chest. "Then I can keep being sweet to you."

"Oh, I have no doubt," she replied. Emily closed her eyes and sighed, feeling warm and content.

Chapter Eleven

Cain poured two cups of coffee and handed one to Emily. They strolled over to the kitchen table to enjoy their drinks before they joined the others outside. It seemed they'd missed breakfast, but there was a plate of fresh muffins and Danishes on the table, so at least they had something to snack on.

He wasn't too upset about not getting food, since he'd spent the time mating and loving on Emily.

The back door slid open as Lamont and Tony sauntered in.

"Well, good morning, love birds," Tony greeted.

"Morning," Cain said. "Sorry we missed breakfast," he lied, giving them a huge grin.

"Yeah right," Tony replied with a snort.

"It's okay," Lamont told him as he joined them at table while Tony continued to the coffee pot. "We do have a few things to talk about, though."

Cain reached over and gripped Emily's hand. "Yes, we do."

"So you two finally made up your minds?" Lamont questioned.

"Yes," Cain answered his dad. "I'm returning to school with Emily. I'll do what I can from there, but I thought we might promote Antonio. We'll come home on the weekends for training and to spend time with you and the Pack but we need to do this."

"I agree," Lamont said. "I've already spoken to Antonio. He's excited for the opportunity."

Of course his Alpha already knew what Cain wanted to

do. He was extremely lucky, not only in finding Emily, but also in having the support of his family.

Tony returned to the table and handed Lamont a mug, then took the seat across from Cain. "I'm leaving for California this morning. I still want to go to the Council compound but I'll be available if needed. I think Antonio is the right choice."

"Good." Cain nodded at his brother. It was a great chance for Tony.

"Being in the city, you're going to be closer to Adam and his Pack, and he's going to need you," Lamont changed the subject.

"You know about what's going on with Christian?" Cain questioned.

"Christian called me this morning. I asked him to wait but he decided to pass the Pack over to Adam," Lamont confirmed. "I have complete faith in Adam, but it won't be easy. Especially since they're still trying to recover the feelings of safety and comfort inside the territory from Mindy's attack."

"I'll do whatever I can," Cain promised.

"I also want you to check in with Riker's Enforcer, Larry," Lamont said. "I don't think he's happy or even safe. This Pack owes him and I plan on doing whatever I can to help that young man. He didn't have to step in to protect Emily but he did."

"You don't plan to ask him to join the Pack, do you?" Cain asked. His Alpha was right, they did owe him, but that didn't mean Cain wanted a daily reminder of what had happened to Emily.

She squeezed his hand and he smiled at her.

"Not right now," Lamont said. "I don't think he'd be happy here, since he would come in without a job or any position. But there are opportunities he might like to take advantage of. There are Packs that are in dire need of a strong second or third."

"But you're still not sure about him," Cain guessed.

Lamont nodded but didn't verbally respond. Cain was actually reassured that he wasn't the only one who still wasn't sure about Larry. "I'll see what I can do."

"Thank you," Lamont told him.

"So when are you going to leave?" Tony asked, after a few minutes of silence.

"In the morning, I think." Cain glanced at Emily who nodded. "We need to get to the city so Emily will be ready to start classes next week and I can make sure I have everything I'll need there. If anything comes up here I can be back in just a couple of hours."

"Sounds good," Lamont said. "It'll seem empty having both of you gone."

Cain frowned. Did his father not want him to go?

"Don't look like that." Lamont pointed a finger at him. "I still have Toby here with me, and the Pack. I won't be alone."

"I know," Cain agreed. He started to run his thumb over Emily's fingers and he knew that he had to keep his promise anyway. She wanted to return to campus and he had to support her.

"We'll be back on the weekends," she said. "I swore to Toby I'd come back more."

Cain smiled. His little brother was determined not to lose Emily again.

"Maybe he can even come up for some visits when he isn't in school," he suggested.

Emily beamed, and Lamont nodded. "I think he'd like that," Lamont said. "But what do you think about taking over the house that Emily usually stays in? When you're here it'll give the two of you more privacy."

Cain hadn't considered moving out of the main house. He could have had any of the cabins at any time, but he'd been comfortable with his family. Still, they would need privacy.

He turned to Emily but she was only looking back at him. "I think it's a good idea," he said. "What about you?"

"I love that house," Emily agreed.

"Okay," Cain said to his dad. "We'll take it."

"We might want to find a new apartment in the city, though. Mine's only a one bedroom and if we got something bigger then you could have an office, and we need a spare room in case Toby or anyone from the Pack visits," Emily suggested.

"Are you sure?" Cain questioned.

She nodded. "I've lived there since I moved to the city but I don't have any attachment to it. At the time it was all I needed. Now we should get something bigger."

"Sure," Cain said. "We'll look before the semester starts and even if I have to move us while you're in class it shouldn't be a problem."

"Then it's settled," Lamont said, standing. "I have a few calls to make but I'll see you at dinner."

"I hate leaving him," Tony said after Lamont had left the kitchen.

"I know, but he wants us to live our lives too," Cain told him.

"I want to go to California," Tony said. "There are talks about the Council considering shifters going public and announcing our existence."

"No way!" Emily exclaimed.

"Wow," Cain agreed. "I can't even imagine. What would we do?"

Tony shook his head. "I don't know. There was an entire Pack in Washington slaughtered by poachers when they were out for a run as a Pack. The hunting laws all over the country are different and we need to find a way to protect our species. All shifters, actually. It's completely legal to kill many species in certain parts and since we stay in animal form if we die while shifted, no one knows how many people have been killed."

"I can see why it needs to be done," Cain said. "But why can't we just have stiffer penalties and laws for hunting instead of exposing our secret?"

His brother shrugged. "It just isn't working. And this is

only an idea. If it does happen then I want to be involved. This isn't something that can be decided quickly and it scares me that the Council is considering it."

"Now I'm even happier you're going," Cain told him.

"Me too," Emily agreed. "It's hard to keep a secret like being a shifter but the alternative is terrifying. I've spent time in a cage and couldn't ever do that again."

She shivered and Cain shifted his chair closer to her so he could wrap his arm around her shoulder. "I would never let that happen again. If there is a threat against us because the Council does decide to go public we would disappear and no one will ever hurt you."

"I know," she said, cuddling into him. "Just the thought of anyone going through even a fraction of what I did is heartbreaking."

"That's why the Council is discussing the announcement. Protection of all shifters is the number one goal. They won't allow anyone to be experimented on or put in danger," Tony said.

"If you don't mind keeping me informed, I would appreciate it," Cain told him.

"Of course," Tony agreed. He pushed back from the table and stood. "I do need to get on the road, though. I'm following behind the two Council representatives that arrived earlier. They're taking Brent back to the Council to stand trial."

"I hope they put him down like a rabid dog," Cain spat.

"I'll make sure of it," Tony promised.

Cain rose and hugged his brother tight. It would be weird not to see Tony every day, but they did need to live their lives, and Tony had so much potential to truly become the best Alpha or a member of the Council. Cain believed that Tony would do great things.

Tony slapped his back several times before stepping away from Cain. "Come give me a hug, little sister," he said to Emily.

She jumped to her feet before wrapping her arms around

his back. Their embrace was a lot shorter than his had been, and Cain appreciated it. He didn't even want his brother to touch his mate.

Cain turned to Emily as Tony made his way out of the room. "What do you say we head over to the cabin and see what we need to make it more comfortable? It's definitely going to need a better coffee pot, since that one only makes four cups at a time."

She laughed, like he wanted, before nodding. "Sure."

He took her hand in his then led her from the kitchen to the back door. He let her pass through first, but quickly followed after. There was a nice breeze and he considered taking the long way to the cabin, but they would have to go through the woods if they went that way, and Cain wasn't ready to face that yet. Soon he would go back to the spot of the unsuccessful attack on Emily but not today.

Without him saying anything, Emily grabbed his arm and led him away from the woods to the path toward the cabins.

Two teenagers were running around passing a football. They stopped long enough to wave at Cain and Emily. Toby was playing on one of the swing sets with a couple of other kids. Cain could picture their own kids out there one day. Toby would be a good uncle and Emily was going to make an amazing mom. He hadn't realized they'd stopped to watch the children until Emily leaned into his side.

"One day," she whispered.

"I can't wait," he told her. "I want time, just me and you, but I can't wait for us to have kids."

"A little boy with your dark hair," she said.

"A little girl with your heart of gold," he corrected.

She laughed. "I guess we'll have both."

Since he didn't want to scare her away, he decided not to mention that he really wanted at least four kids. There was plenty of time for him to broach the subject. "Come on," Cain encouraged with a nudge.

As they walked down the street, he could see the porch of the cabin come into view. He knew how much Emily loved that area of the place, and one of the first things he was going to order was some nice furniture that she could sit on outside and enjoy the territory.

One of the older residents stepped out of her porch and smiled at them as they passed.

"Hi, Mrs. Johnson," Emily called out.

"Hello, children," she replied.

Cain waved.

The concrete steps were still in good shape and the paint was fairly new so there wasn't anything he needed to do outside. Emily jogged in front of him to the front door and turned the knob to open it.

"You need to lock it from now on," he told her as he stepped up behind her.

"Really?" She glanced over her shoulder. "We're in the middle of the territory."

He shook his head. "Doesn't matter. From now on, always lock up."

"Yes, sir." She gave him a sarcastic salute but was grinning.

Cain headed toward the kitchen to brew more coffee. He hadn't been kidding about needing a better machine, but he'd take care of that later. The kitchen walls were painted in a light tan color, which looked really good against the wood cabinets. "Is there anything that you want done inside? I can hire some of the guys to remodel whatever we need."

Emily turned in a circle as she stood in the entry. "Not really. I love everything about this place. The bedroom and bathroom are perfect. We might want to paint the living room though, since it's white, but I can't really think of anything I don't like."

"Okay," he agreed. "You can pick the color and I'll have it done."

Emily took a seat at the table while Cain went about filling the water reserve.

"Do you want a bigger apartment or should we look for a

house while we live away from here?" he asked her. He had plenty of money saved up, plus he would still be getting his income from the Pack, so he could get her a house if that was what she wanted.

"Apartment," she answered immediately.

"Really? We'd have more room in a house," Cain said.

"If we bought one we'd just sell it after I finished school. I have no desire to live in the city once I have my degree," Emily told him.

"We could rent a house close to campus," he suggested.

"Then we'd have to keep up with home repairs and the lawn. If we're coming back here every weekend then we already have to do that here. Why make extra work for us? We'll both be busy," she said.

Yeah, she had a good point. "We can find a three bedroom then."

"I'd like that. I do want Toby to visit and if you'd like to set up some training in the city it would be a good idea to have a spare room," she said.

"Training," he repeated. All of the guards lived and worked on the property so it might be wise to get them out of their comfort zone. Especially if what Tony said about maybe going public was true. He needed to start thinking outside the box when it came to preparing. "Yeah."

He began to pace as he worked out what he could set up. Cain would need to get more familiar with the city and whatever neighborhood they moved into, but he had no doubt his father would think it was a good idea too. "I like that. Good idea."

She smiled and it was obvious to him that she was pleased he'd listened to her suggestion. Cain sauntered across the room and towered over her. He gripped her ponytail and tugged her head back gently.

"You're going to have to keep sharing your ideas with me. We have to take care of our Pack," he said.

Emily grabbed the front of his shirt and yanked him back down so their mouths slammed together. Cain licked her bottom lip until she opened for him and he could plunge his tongue inside. He bent his knees so he could grip her legs then lifted her.

"That's better," he said, once he'd lifted his mouth from hers. He sat her on top of the table with her ass on the edge.

She'd dressed in soft gray pants and a white tank top. He ran his hands from her knees up to her thighs before pressing his middle finger against her covered pussy.

"Mmm," Emily moaned as she let her head fall back.

Cain dropped into the chair that he'd just taken her from and pulled her to the edge. He hadn't shaved that morning so he knew she'd be able to feel his stubble through her thin pants as he rubbed all over her crotch.

"Oh God! I want your mouth on me," she told him.

"Lift up," he ordered.

Emily flung her flip-flops off before planting her feet on the table so she could raise her hips. He tugged the waistband of her pants down, making sure to collect her panties as well. He flung them to the side then spread her legs with his hands.

"Please," she said, arching her back.

He swiped his tongue through her folds, tasting her sweet pussy.

"Cain!" she cried out.

He added a finger with his tongue until she was pushing against him. She ran her hands over the back of his head, holding him down as she bucked and began to plead.

Cain thrust a second finger inside her while covering her clit with his mouth and sucking. Emily shouted and came, clutching his head so hard she might've pulled out some of his hair.

"Good, so good," she mumbled as she started to calm down.

He jumped to his feet, trying to get his jeans undone with his hands shaking.

"Get up here," she demanded. "I want you to fuck my mouth."

"Shit!" He seized the base of his cock and squeezed to keep from coming. Emily had him so worked up that he just about lost it.

"I mean it, Cain," she said. "Come here."

"Damn," he muttered. "Hang on." He had to hop around and to get his boots and socks off before he shoved his jeans down his legs. He climbed up onto the table with her. He sure the hell hoped that it would hold both their weights. This probably wasn't the best idea but he wasn't about to try to get her into the bedroom. If he didn't get release soon he felt like he'd die.

As soon as he was in reach, Emily captured his cock in a light hold and directed him to straddle her head. He placed his hands on either side of her as he lowered himself.

She opened her mouth and sucked on the tip a little before he rocked his hips, letting more of his shaft go in. As much as he wanted to ram and drive his cock deep and have her swallow around him, he didn't. It wasn't going to take much to get him to come and he had to maintain control.

Emily hummed then lifted her neck and forced him deeper. He tried to pull back, but she gripped his ass hard and he thrust deeper than he meant to.

"Fuck!" She didn't choke, just patted his ass while tonguing his cock. It felt like she was tracing the veins of his shaft.

He withdrew until only the tip remained, then slid back in over and over. Every time a little faster and deeper, until he had to tear himself away.

She whimpered and reached out, but he shook his head. "I want to mark you," he told her. "Please, please let me."

"Yes," she told him and lay back down flat.

Cain stroked his cock until he climaxed, pointing his shaft at Emily's breasts and stomach.

He about passed out when she reached down and started to rub her clit while he painted her with his seed. "Jesus! Yes! Get off again!"

Emily spread her legs even wider then screamed, reaching

orgasm. He moved so his cum landed on her fingers and she was rubbing his fluid into her clit until they were both spent. He was barely able to avoid crushing her as he fell to the side.

What a sight they probably made, both naked and covered in semen while lying on the kitchen table.

"Remind me to buy Lysol wipes," he mumbled.

She giggled, and snorted, then laughed louder. He couldn't even try not to laugh right along with her. "Just think, we'll have a whole apartment to christen."

"I think you might just kill me," he said, throwing an arm over his eyes. "Wake me in an hour."

* * * *

"You sure you didn't forget anything?" Cain asked Emily as he opened the driver door and climbed out.

"Yep," she said laughing. "And it's not like we won't be back there in a few days if I did."

"Okay." He strolled around to the back of the silver Cadillac Escalade ESV that his father had gifted him and Emily with earlier that morning. Both he and Emily had tried to tell him that they didn't need such an expensive vehicle, but Lamont had called it a mating gift and had said they needed a reliable SUV for driving back and forth from the city to the Pack.

Cain could admit that the interior was pure luxury and he really liked the heated leather seats. Emily had spent the first twenty minutes playing with all the buttons. It would have been even longer, but he'd threatened to tie her hands if she didn't stop. The gleam in her eyes had had him hardening fast and he'd almost pulled over to the side of the road and taken her, but he'd resisted.

He glanced up at her apartment building, much like he'd done when he'd come to pick her up so recently.

The last time he'd stared up into the entry of her apartment he'd been preparing himself to see her again. Now he was returning with her and he felt complete.

"You okay?" she asked, coming to his side with her bags.

Cain turned his head so he could kiss her. "Yeah, just thinking."

"Well, stop that," she said. "Let's get inside and order some food. I'm too tired to cook and there are some really good restaurants around here that deliver."

"Sounds like a plan," he agreed. Cain strolled back to the SUV and picked up his two bags before slamming the back closed.

She was waiting for him at the stairs, so he hurried over to her.

"You sure you're not going to miss this place?" he asked as they started to climb up.

"I am," she replied. "I like it, but any place we live together will be better."

He nodded even though she was in front of him and couldn't see. "I want to try to find something fairly quickly. That way I can get a training schedule set up. Lamont loved the idea of bringing the guards down here to expand their experience."

They'd reached her front door and he had to wait as Emily searched through her bag for her keys.

"Uh ha!" she exclaimed, pulling them out. She unlocked and opened the door before waving him through. "Our home, at least until you find us a new one."

He grinned as he passed her. "I'm going to drop my stuff in the bedroom."

"Go ahead," she called out behind him.

The place wasn't big, but he could see why she was comfortable there. The building was modernized and well-kept, but it was small and he would need his own space. When she went to campus to pick up her books and do whatever else she needed, he was going to call a realtor. The only stipulation she'd had was that she was still close to campus. He was certain they would find something that would fit their needs.

Cain dropped his bags by the door and turned to find Emily when his cell rang. He dug the device out of his pocket, surprised to see Adam's name on the display.

"Hey, man," Cain greeted.

"Hey, did you get to the city all right?" Adam asked.

Cain had texted Adam earlier, telling his friend that Cain would be close by in case Adam needed anything. "Just got in, as matter of fact."

"Good," Adam replied. "I'm glad you're going to be close by."

"Me too," Cain said. "Don't think you have to do everything alone. We're here to help."

"I know." Adam sounded down.

"What's wrong?" he pressed.

There were several seconds of silence so Cain pulled his phone away to make sure he hadn't lost connection.

"Adam?"

"My dad's inner circle would like to retire. They think it would be better if I made my own and had people that I could trust and grow with the Pack," Adam told him.

"But they're not leaving, are they?" Cain asked.

"No, and they're willing to help and stand as advisors, but this gives them the opportunity to spend more time with their families. I understand, but it's a lot to take in at once."

"I understand," Cain said. There were so many changes happening, and while Adam had his family he was taking on a lot of responsibility.

"I know I can care for my Pack," Adam said. "I don't have any doubts about that, but I don't know where to start."

"All you can do is take everything one step at a time," Cain suggested. "Make a list of what you want or need to do. Then prioritize the list. It will all work out, and don't be afraid to depend on your friends. Especially mine and Gage's. I can even send some of my guards if you need me to. I'm sure Gage would be more than willing to as well."

"I've been approached already by several of the shifters

that would like to be trained. There are more than a few that I would like to see move up if they're willing to work hard."

"See," Cain said. "Things are already starting to work out."

"First, I need to find an Enforcer so I have a second and someone to train the new guards. I asked the Council for recommendations. If you can think of anyone who might be interested let me know," Adam requested.

"I'll think on it. We might have someone who wants to move up," Cain said. He couldn't think of anyone off the top of his head, but maybe Emily would have an idea as well.

"Thanks, man."

Cain could hear someone start to talk to Adam and his friend sighed.

"Sorry, I have to run, but maybe I can get up to the city and we can have lunch. I haven't gotten to see Emily much and would love to hear how you two are doing," Adam said.

"We'd like that. We'll talk later," Cain replied.

"Okay, see you."

Cain disconnected the call and lifted his head. Emily leaned against the threshold to the bedroom smiling at him.

"Adam doing okay?" she asked, strolling closer.

He held out a hand to her. "I think so. He has a lot of work to do, but he's ready for this."

Emily sat on his lap. "And you? Are you ready to live with me full-time?"

"Yes," Cain assured her. "I'm looking forward to waking up with you in my arms every morning and kissing you goodnight before we sleep."

"So sweet," she teased before laying her cheek against his. "But don't worry I won't tell anyone."

He laughed and embraced her tighter. It wasn't going to be easy learning how to give up some of his control and become a full partner to the woman he loved, but he was going to do his damn best. He'd made so many mistakes with Emily, but she had decided he deserved another chance and he was going to prove to her that he would never let her down again.

They belonged together — whether it was fate or something else didn't matter. Emily was his and he was hers.

Epilogue

Adam White stretched his arms out, loosening his muscles as he walked up the back steps to the Alpha house. *His* house now that he'd taken over the Pack from his father. As hard as he'd fought for his dad to remain as the Pack's leader, he also felt a deep connection with the land and his shifters and he wanted to do right by all of them. The stress of the past several months was starting to get to him, but the freedom of being able to shift and run the boundaries of his territory made each hard day worth it.

The late-night run in his other form had done a remarkable job of relaxing him.

Opening the sliding glass door to enter the house, Adam took a deep breath and sensed the interior. He was learning quickly how to use his heightened senses and the bond with his Pack to know where and how they were.

His sister Laura was in the kitchen, baking for the family and other guests who were sure to stop by first thing in the morning. He smiled at the smell of cakes and cookies. His sister always cooked enough food for an army, and his mouth watered in anticipation. If he didn't have the self-control he did, Adam would weigh five hundred pounds.

He took another breath and found the man he was searching for. His father and former Pack Alpha was in his room. Adam wasn't surprised. Christian spent all of his time either in his bedroom or in his wolf form. Adam had tried to talk to him, to bring him out of the depression, but nothing he said or did helped.

Three months before, one of the young females of the Pack had been attacked. Mindy hadn't been the first or the only girl, but she was the only one from *their* Pack. Christian had to live with the knowledge that he hadn't been able to protect a Pack member.

Adam, Laura and many Pack members—even other Alphas—had told Christian it wasn't his fault, but he continued to blame himself.

The only person who seemed to be able reach Christian at all was his friend, Logan.

Logan had been staying at the house and talking with Christian daily, slowly bringing him back. But when Logan's Alpha, Gage, had found out that his mate was pregnant, Logan had had to leave and return to his own territory. As expected, Gage's Pack was on high alert to make certain nothing happened to the Alpha's mate or child. Adam could understand the need, but he selfishly wished Logan could have stayed longer.

Adam headed to his office.

For now, at least, his father was alive. Adam just needed to make sure he remained that way. It wasn't unusual for shifters to want to end their existence after a tragedy. Living for so long and witnessing so much affected each of them.

Opening the door to the Alpha's office, Adam stepped inside and flipped on the light. He had taken his new position only two months before and hadn't changed anything in the office or the house. He didn't know if he even wanted to, though several friends had suggested it would help the transition if he properly claimed the space and made it his own.

Sometimes, Adam still felt like he was playing dress-up and his father would walk back into the office and demand Adam stop messing around.

Intellectually, he knew that wouldn't happen, but it was something he struggled with daily.

The Council, made up of former Alphas who policed the Packs, had given their blessing for him to take over the Pack. His Alpha position was official.

It was a huge responsibility and he didn't want to

disappoint anyone, especially his father. So he worked hard and tried to get everything done while still staying available for the Pack. He'd had no idea the hours an Alpha put in before he'd taken over.

As Adam grew up, his father had always been there for him and had made running the Pack look so easy. Adam was finding out that there was a lot that went on behind the scenes that he'd never known.

He needed help taking care of all those under his protection. But even after a couple months of searching he'd yet to appoint his second-in-command and it weighed heavy on his mind.

He'd thought long and hard about who would be good for the position. Every Alpha picked his own man to watch his back. His father's man had stayed when Adam had taken over, but Adam knew he was more than ready to retire. Their agreement was that he'd train the new second, but he did want to spend more time with his family soon.

As he reached the desk, he turned on the computer and waited for it to boot up. As he sat, there was a knock on the door. He tried not to be annoyed at the interruption, but it was hard. He'd been hoping to have a little time to himself at the late hour. He wanted to finish going through the applications for his Enforcer. There was no one strong enough or dominant enough in his Pack, so he was going to have to bring someone else in.

The Council and several other Packs had sent recommendations but Adam hadn't found anyone who he felt completely comfortable with. An Alpha had to have a second. This person would be Adam's most trusted ally. And he'd been struggling to find the right match.

The knock sounded again, and Adam realized he'd gotten lost in his own thoughts. "Come in!" he called out to the guard that would be on duty.

Tasha Johnson had followed the guard inside the Alpha's house and down the hall. When they'd reached a large oak door, she'd run her sweaty palms over her jeans. She hated to bring her family problems to the new Alpha, but she didn't know where else to turn.

The low voice that told them to enter sent a shiver down her spine. She braced herself as the guard opened the door and nodded at her to stay outside. Procedure dictated that she wait while she was announced, then the Alpha decided whether or not to grant her an audience. Tasha wasn't too worried. Like his father before him, Adam was already known for making time for members of his Pack. As the guard walked from the office, she peeked inside and got a good look at the new Pack leader.

She'd known Adam for years, even though they'd never been close, and had admired him from a distance for a long time now. The fact that she was about to face him alone made her stomach flutter with nerves. He was just so good looking and she did not want to make a fool of herself in front of him. Plus, she really did need his help.

Adam nodded as the guard spoke quietly to him before looking up and locking gazes with her. His light green eyes held hers, and her breath rushed out of her chest at the intensity with which he watched her.

Then he smiled and liquid arousal pooled inside her panties. She shifted to relieve the pressure, certain if she didn't calm her body, he would be able to tell. Oh, the man just oozed raw sexuality.

When he stood and motioned her in, she didn't miss the large bulge trapped in his jeans. The sight of his excitement did nothing to tame her own desire. She wasn't sure if he was reacting to her or not, but a woman could hope. Secretly, she wished he wanted her as much as she did him. Not that she believed that would ever happen. No one with Adam's looks or power would be interested in a nobody like her.

The guard left the office without another word and closed the door behind him. The Alpha's scent surrounded her, and Tasha struggled not to close her eyes and breathe deeply. She had serious business to discuss.

"Bryan told me that you had a family emergency and needed my help," Adam said as he gestured for her to sit.

Weak-kneed, Tasha gladly took a seat on the worn brown leather couch and clasped her hands in her lap. She should be concentrating on getting her sister back instead of her desire for a male. "Yes, Alpha. I need to talk you about my sister, Crystal."

He sat in the chair across from her and leaned forward. "I'm listening. Whatever you need I'll help."

"I'm not sure if your father told you about my family when you took over the Pack." She was so nervous, she could feel sweat bead on her forehead. She hated talking about her family and sharing the pain of her past.

She could see the sympathy in his eyes when he spoke. "Why don't you tell me?"

Tasha took a deep breath before starting. "Five years ago, my father left our family. I'm still not sure where he went, but my mother didn't take it well. Six months after he left, she ended her existence and left Crystal with me. She was eleven."

He nodded but didn't comment. She appreciated him letting her get the story out quickly. The sooner she finished, the sooner she could once again bury her pain.

"I've tried to do the best I can, but I don't always understand what she is going through. My sister Crystal is a…non-shifter." Tasha waited for his reaction. Being a non-shifter was an embarrassment for her sister. Tasha only saw how wonderful her sibling was instead of whether she could shift or not, and even though she didn't understand, she always respected Crystal's wishes. They didn't tell many people because a lot of Pack members considered non-shifters lower class.

"Go on," he told her gently, and she didn't hear or see anything negative from him.

"Crystal's had a hard time lately with some of the kids from school. That's why I think she ran away."

"Do you have any idea where she could have gone?" he asked, and Tasha just stared at him. Didn't he want to ask questions about the non-shifter part of the story? He didn't say anything more, instead simply waited for her reply.

"I do. I talked to her best friend and she told me that Crystal has been talking to a boy in the city over the Internet. She probably went there." Tasha spoke quickly. "I have his name and number. I keep trying to call but no one is answering. He is older and I'm worried about what he might do to her."

Adam leaned over and placed his hand over hers. "Give me the information and I will find her. I promise you that."

Tasha could feel tears threaten to fall in relief. "Thank you, Alpha. Thank you."

He squeezed her hand before releasing it. "That is what I am here for. Do you have the information with you?"

Tasha nodded and dug in her purse for her small notebook. Her hand still tingled from where Adam had touched her. "I wrote it all down." She tore out a page and handed it to him, hoping he didn't notice her hands shaking.

"I'll work on this and let you know what I find out," he told her as he stood. He reached down and helped her stand.

She bit back her moan when his touch caused her body once again to tingle. Her breasts felt fuller and heavy, her stomach tightened, and her sex clinched. It was unbelievable how much she could want one man.

They stood close, not quite touching, and stared at each other for several minutes. Adam shook his head and took a step back. "I'll be in touch."

Tasha turned and took a deep cleansing breath. She needed to get a hold of herself. It would be wrong to throw herself at her Alpha's feet and beg him to take her.

"Thank you," she murmured as she made her way to the door.

Hell, with wolf senses, he could do a lot more than just hear well. There was no doubt in her mind that he knew just how much she wanted him. Then again, she was also a wolf shifter. His need had saturated the room.

She left the room with a small smile on her face. It felt like way too long since she'd had anything to smile about.

Pack Territory

Excerpt

Chapter One

Adam White stretched his arms out as he walked up the back steps to his house. The late night run in his other form had done a remarkable job of relaxing him.

Opening the sliding glass door to enter the house, Adam took a deep breath and sensed the interior. His sister Laura was in the kitchen baking for the family and other guests who were sure to stop in. He smiled at the smell of cakes and cookies. His sister always cooked enough food for an army, and his mouth watered in anticipation.

He calmly took another breath and found the man he was searching for. His father and former Pack Alpha was in his room. Adam wasn't surprised. Christian spent all of his time either in his room or in his other form. Adam had tried to talk to him, to bring him out of the depression, but nothing he said or did helped.

Three months before, one of the young females of the Pack had been attacked. Mindy hadn't been the first or the only girl, but she was the only one from their Pack. Christian had to live with the knowledge that he hadn't been able to protect a Pack member.

Adam, Laura, and many Pack members—even other Alphas—had told Christian it wasn't his fault, but he continued to blame himself. The only person who seemed to be able reach him at all was his friend, Logan.

Logan had been staying at the house and talking with Christian daily, slowly bringing him back. But when Logan's Alpha, Gage, had found out that his mate was pregnant, Logan had to leave and return to his own territory. As expected, Gage's Pack was in high alert to make certain nothing happened to the Alpha's mate or child. Adam could understand the need, but he selfishly wished Logan could have stayed longer.

Adam headed to his office. For now, at least, his father was alive. Adam just needed to make sure he remained that way. It wasn't unusual for shifters to want to end their existence after a tragedy. Living for so long and witnessing so much affected each of them.

Opening the door to the Alpha's office, Adam stepped inside and flipped on the light. He had taken his new position only two months before and hadn't changed anything in the office or the house. He didn't know if he ever would.

The council, made up of former Alphas who policed the Packs, had given their blessing for him to take over the Pack, but Adam still had doubts whether he was ready. It was a huge responsibility and he didn't want to disappoint anyone, especially his father. The fact that he still needed to appoint his second-in-command weighed heavy on his mind.

He'd thought long and hard about who would be good for the position. Every Alpha picked his own man to watch his back. His father's man had stayed when Adam took over, but Adam knew he was more than ready to retire.

As he reached the desk, he turned on the computer and waited for it to boot up. As he sat, there was a knock on the door. He tried not to be annoyed at the interruption, but it was hard. He'd been hoping to have a little time to himself at the late hour. He wanted to finish going through the applications for his Enforcer. He had put it off long enough.

More books from Crissy Smith

The Rogue meets the Alpha…and their worlds explode.

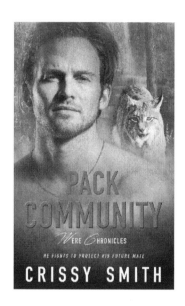

A wolf and bobcat come together and change one community, forever.

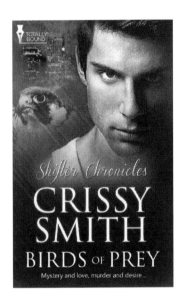

Mystery and love, murder and desire… It's going to be a rough week for the agents of the Birds of Prey shifter division.

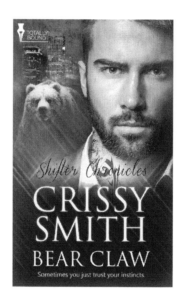

Shifter Chronicles

CRISSY SMITH

BEAR CLAW

Sometimes you just trust your instincts.

Beauty and grace meet muscles and tattoos. When what's on the outside doesn't match the inside, sometimes you just trust your instincts.

About the Author

Crissy Smith

Crissy Smith lives in Texas with her husband, daughter, and three Labrador retrievers. The three dogs love to curl up under her computer desk and nap while she writes. It doesn't leave a lot of room for her but what's a woman to do?

When not writing or reading, she enjoys hunting, camping and shooting. But she has a girly side too and is addicted to pedicures and coffee.

She has been writing since she was a teenager and still loves everything to do with the paranormal. Her stories and characters all have a place in her heart. She loves the alpha male, the dominant werewolf, or the Master vampire which find their way in most of her books.

Learn more about the characters she has created at her website where they have their very own page. It will be updated from time to time to let you know what's going on with them. Also you can find out who will be in the next book.

Crissy Smith loves to hear from readers. You can find contact information, website details and an author profile page at https://www.totallybound.com/

Home of Erotic Romance

18461635R00103

Printed in Great Britain
by Amazon